CHRISTMAS DREAMS

SOUL SISTERS AT CEDAR MOUNTAIN LODGE

EV BISHOP

CHRISTMAS DREAMS

Copyright © 2020 Ev Bishop

Trade Paperback Edition

Published by Winding Path Books

ISBN: 978-1-77265-048-8

Cover image: Elizabeth Mackey

www.elizabethmackeygraphics.com

Christmas Dreams is a work of fiction. Names, characters, places, and incidents are either the product of the author's imagination or are used fictitiously, and any resemblance to actual persons, living or dead, business establishments, events or locales is entirely coincidental.

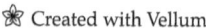 Created with Vellum

For Laura and Jo, my real-life soul sisters, with so much love.

ALSO BY EV BISHOP

Bigger Things

A Sharla Brown Christmas

Wedding Bands (River's Sigh B & B, Book 1)

Hooked (River's Sigh B & B, Book 2)

Spoons (River's Sigh B & B, Book 3)

Hook, Line & Sinker (River's Sigh B & B, Book 4)

Silver Bells (River's Sigh B & B, Book 5)

Reeling (River's Sigh B & B, Book 6)

New Year's Resolution: One to Keep (River's Sigh B & B, Book 7)

The Catch (River's Sigh B & B, Book 8)

River's Sigh B & B Vol. 1 – 4

River's Sigh B & B Vol. 5 – 8

Writing as Toni Sheridan

The Present

Drummer Boy

Visit www.evbishop.com for more information about upcoming
works, to sign up for *Ev's News*, or to drop Ev a line.

PROLOGUE

Her jaw was clenched so tightly that her teeth ached, but Stevie thought that was probably preferable to standing there with her hands balled into fists, looking like she wanted to punch somebody.

Her latest social worker, Natalie, a hideously cheerful woman who always insisted that whatever new family she stuck Stevie into could be "the one," pressed the ornate, old-fashioned doorbell. A series of musical chimes rang somewhere deep inside the house. While they waited for Mrs. Kirby to answer the door—still so weird that her guidance counselor was going to be her foster mom—Stevie studied the fancy Victorian mansion in front of her. And that's what it was—a *mansion*. Mrs. Kirby called it a "house," but it was definitely more than that.

Beside Stevie were Hailey and Alissa, two young girls she'd just been informed were also going to be staying with Mrs. Kirby. They fidgeted and craned their necks to look around—but were absolutely silent. Stevie figured their stomachs were probably churning with the same emotions as hers: anger mixed with sprinkles of awe and heavy dollops of fear.

Eight-years-old and ten-years-old respectively, Hailey and

Alissa were extraordinarily petite. They were like little fairies, unfairly placed in a cold, unfamiliar world—one dark-haired, one strawberry blond with coke bottle thick glasses. Stevie's heart went out to them, much good as that ever did anyone. Her jaw clenched harder. Yes, Mrs. Kirby was a good person. But there was only so much even the *best* person could do, and the moment Natalie introduced Alissa and Hailey to Stevie and mentioned they were being fostered by Mrs. Kirby too, Stevie's hope withered into a blackened, stringy thing. And *that* had surprised her—that she'd actually *had* a small tender morsel of hope in the first place. Was she totally stupid or what? She'd really thought she knew better by now. She wanted to say something reassuring to Hailey and Alissa. They were quiet, cute as buttons, and *young*. They stood a chance of finding a forever home, especially compared to her, but she said nothing. Little kids weren't idiots, and from the bit Natalie said—and what she didn't say—Stevie gleaned that these two had both been in the system a while already, hence their wariness. It didn't matter how cute or sweet you were. There was no rhyme or reason to why some kids were born into love, or, at least, into families with the ability and desire to care for their offspring, while others got the opposite of those things. In fact, it was probably better—or safer, anyway—if you were a bit of an asshole like she was. At least she didn't get messed with.

Stevie realized she had clenched her fists, after all. She forced them open and tried to look chill as the big shiny red door opened. Cozy heat and warm golden light spilled into the frigid evening air. And haloed by all that light was Mrs. Kirby herself, smiling and welcoming them in like she was genuinely excited they'd arrived.

"Finally," she exclaimed. "You're here!"

Stevie smiled despite her nerves. It was such a relief to be ushered inside. A huge part of her had been sure Mrs. Kirby would change her mind, positive her question that day in her office all those weeks ago, "How would you feel about coming to live with me?" had been asked out of kindness, not any sincere desire. And yet here Stevie was, days before Christmas, walking into a house that would've been the perfect setting for a Christmas movie, carrying all her worldly possessions. She hated herself for being so weak, but honestly, even if staying with Mrs. Kirby didn't last long, it was better than the alternative—one that she knew better than to share with anyone. She was done with temporary placements and crappy group homes. There was a good chance her mom, AKA Marilyn, would show up again at some point. And if not? Well, she'd get a job or something. She had friends with street smarts—the only upside of the foster system, in her opinion. They'd help her find a place to squat until she could buy a secondhand car or something more permanent to stay in. She was only thirteen, but so what? Age was just a state of mind, right? That's what Marilyn said all the time, anyway.

"Are you going to come in, Stevie, or do you need a minute alone?"

Stevie startled. She'd done that thing that so often got her into trouble at school: disappeared into her head. She wasn't ignoring anyone or being "willfully disrespectful."

She was just—doing it again. Rats!

She swallowed and tried to speak. Nothing came out. She cleared her throat and tried again. Successfully this time. "I'll come in. Something smells really good. Thank you."

"It's roast chicken with veggies and mashed potatoes," Mrs. Kirby said as if it was no big deal. "I hope you're hungry."

Stevie was always hungry.

Dinner surprised Stevie by not being as awkward as she feared. The food was delicious—and plentiful. Mrs. Kirby, who asked them to call her Maddie, insisted they should eat as much as they wanted—and seemed to mean it. She smiled when Stevie gobbled up seconds, then thirds, of creamy potatoes with to-die-for gravy. And when Stevie asked, "Is this gravy homemade?" Maddie gave a full-on grin. "You bet. I can teach you how to make it sometime if you want."

Stevie did want that. She wanted that a lot—and even if it would never come to pass, it was very kind of Maddie to offer.

There was another girl at Mrs. Kirby's too, a fifteen-year-old named Jo, who'd arrived the night before. Jo was the type of girl that Stevie found intimidating at school: well-spoken, tall and slim, and somehow polished and put together looking, even though, at a second glance, her clothes were almost as ragged as Stevie's. She seemed nice, though—and smiled shyly at Stevie more than once, which was not how most pretty, obviously smart older girls usually reacted to her baggy jeans, gray sweatshirt, board shoe wearing self. At best, she was invisible to them. At worst—well, there was no "worst" anymore. They'd learned the hard way to leave her alone.

The rest of the evening was surprisingly comfortable too. Stevie had stayed at places where after meals, heck, *during* meals, people were as silent and expressionless as stones—and about as friendly. But Maddie was the same way in her home that she was at school. She had this gentle, no-pressure way of letting you talk or not, whatever you were more comfortable with, that Stevie appreciated, and that put them all at ease. And she told funny stories and asked interesting questions but didn't try too hard.

When no one could eat another bite, Jo offered to help with the dishes, and Stevie got up too, starting to clear plates.

Maddie insisted she didn't need any help with the dishes, saying she'd take care of them later, adding lightly that maybe there would be a chore chart or something in the future.

Stevie was crestfallen. Maybe it was dumb, but she wanted to do the dishes—wanted to give back in some little way, to not just be a total freeloader. Maddie must have sensed as much because she nodded Stevie's way. "Of course, if you really *want* to load the dishwasher, you can, but tonight's supposed to be a special treat. I don't want you to feel any pressure."

Stevie knew it was stupid, but she practically jumped up from the table.

There was something very weird and nice about doing dishes while other people chatted in a friendly, homey way. Maddie outlined possible plans for the next few days, including going shopping in town for little gifts for each other. Then she suggested, almost shyly, that it was her family's tradition—one she'd like to continue if they were game— to write letters to Santa.

Write a letter to Santa? Stevie hadn't written a letter to Santa since, well, since she was much smaller than Alissa and Hailey, put it that way.

But she felt so grateful to be in this cozy place, surrounded by greenery, twinkling lights, and not just one but *two* huge Christmas trees, that she couldn't help but get caught up in the excitement that Alissa and Hailey were obviously feeling.

As they were getting paper and picking pen colors, Jo caught Stevie's eye and quirked one eyebrow the tiniest bit, not rudely and not in a making fun of Maddie way, but just enough to say, "I know, right? Pretty weird!"

And it was a bit weird, yes, but it was also just one more thing to like about Maddie. That she saw the four of them, a collection of unwanted mutts, as people who should get to do something as simple and fun as write to Santa. That she would act like there might actually be a chance, any chance at all, for the four of them to have wishes that came true.

They each settled in various parts of the house to write. Stevie chose the "family room," which, as far as Stevie could tell, was just a word you used when you had more than one "living room" and needed to distinguish between the similar spaces. Initially, the huge armchair set near a legit, one 100 percent real fireplace that crackled cheerily away seemed the perfect place to pen a note. Now, however, contemplating the sheet of ivory stationery lying atop the hardcovered book she was using as a makeshift desk, Stevie wished she hadn't just loaded the dishwasher. She should've scrubbed the pots and pans too. Anything would be better than staring at a blank page.

She chewed the end of her purple-inked pen lightly, then caught herself and stopped. She didn't want Maddie to think she was mistreating her property.

Okay, here goes nothing, Stevie finally decided. With great resolve, she bowed her head and joined the other girls who were quietly scribbling away in various cozy spots around the big Christmas tree.

Dear Santa,

You already know who I am, but in case you've forgotten (as the jaded side of me says you obviously have), my name is Stevie Fox. I am thirteen. I am staying at Mrs. Madeline Kirby's house for a while. She's my guidance counselor at school and is the person who figured out my mom bailed (again). She didn't think it was "appropriate" for me to live alone in our apartment and called social services. Not gonna lie. It kind of pissed me off, but I get she was just doing her job. Also, rent was due, and since I had (have!) no money, I would've gotten busted anyway.

Her husband and daughter were killed in an accident. I heard some teachers talking about it at the gossip factory, aka my school. That's only relevant because it makes me think she knows how life can really suck and how there's nothing you can do about it. Also, it makes me feel like things could be worse. My mom isn't dead, after all.

Maddie (she asked us to call her that, so I'm not being disrespectful) also noticed that every foster home and group home I got stuck in sucked worse than the last one.

It's weird that I'm looking forward to Christmas this year. I'm okay if it lets me down, but I really hope it will be nice for the other girls, especially Hailey and Alissa because they're little.

Stevie contemplated her cramped handwriting, forced herself not to cross anything out, and flipped the page. Jo, who was also nestled in the family room, almost out of view beside the big Christmas tree, still seemed to be writing, so Stevie wrote some more, too.

Maddie said this thing at dinner about being grateful. It kind of freaked me out—that she would still be grateful after everything she's been through. She's a good person, and anyone who gets to stay with her long term is super lucky. I know that's not me, and I get it, but I'll try to follow her example anyway. I'm grateful that I'm here right now. I already know I'm going to be a really hard worker and that I'll be able to take care of myself, but getting to stay at Maddie's, even for a little while, is a much-needed break.

Sincerely,

Stevie Fox

P.S. Maddie says we're supposed to ask for something. I don't cook very much, but I think I would like to. Food is good—makes you grow and all that (though I'll probably always be a short dwarf), but even better, it makes me feel good. And when you eat with other people, it just feels . . . good. (I'm sorry I keep using the word "good" so much. My English teacher would definitely give me marks off for not being specific, but you're Santa and this isn't for marks, so SUCK IT, Mr. B!!!) Anyway, back to the point. I think you've eaten enough milk and cookies in your life, that you probably have a really kick-ass cookie recipe. So yeah, I would like your favorite Christmas cookie recipes. Yeah, that's right. It being Christmas, this being a wish list, I am asking for not just one cookie recipe, but all your faves. (Ha ha! I'm so greedy, hey?)

P.P.S. I totally get it if you can't share your recipes with me. No worries.

It was late when they finished their Christmas letters, so Maddie took them on a tour of the rest of the house, including their sleeping arrangements.

Even though Stevie didn't know Jo very well at all, the second-floor room Maddie chose for her seemed perfect. It looked like a study—or what she imagined a "study" to look like having only ever read about them in books. Jo looked shyly excited too, and Stevie's stomach squeezed with happiness. It was nice when something worked out.

Then Maddie showed Alissa and Hailey their bedroom, also on the second floor. She said she thought they might enjoy rooming together more than being alone in separate rooms, and from their matching smiles and the little giggle that Hailey let out, she was right.

While the other girls washed up and brushed their teeth, Maddie pulled Stevie aside. "The room I have in mind for you is on the main floor like mine."

Stevie had no idea what to expect and swallowed hard as she followed Maddie back downstairs, then toward a heavy oak door that opened just off the kitchen of all things.

Maddie's hand rested on the door's small antique knob, but she didn't open it right away. "This room is a bit . . . unique. I think it was a pantry of some kind, but that it also did double duty as a room for kitchen help or a live-in maid or something." Maddie laughed. "Not that I'm implying I expect or want you to be my maid. I just thought there was something, I don't know, sort of homey or nostalgic about the room that you, with all the reading you do, might appreciate. The bed is built into the back wall, and there's a big old apple barrel beside it—over one hundred years old. It kind of amazes me. Through all the renovations and changes in owners this house has seen, no one ever got rid of. And the room still smells softly of apples, even after all these years. Plus, there's a big built-in bureau—"

Maddie interrupted herself with a gusty inhale. "I'm talking your ear off! Just come and have a peek."

Stevie's mind reeled. She honestly would've slept on a pullout in Maddie's living room and thought herself awesomely lucky. She fully expected the "unique" room to be great because how could any space in this house not be—and yet she was still unprepared for the burst of emotions that sizzled through her when Maddie clicked on a light and Stevie followed her over the threshold. She gasped.

"Are you all right?" Genuine concern laced Maddie's voice.

Stevie could only nod. Then she felt a smile start all the way down in her belly and spread through her body with a tingle. She understood what Maddie meant; it did look like it had probably been servants' quarters at some time in history —but quarters designed by someone who had appreciated their servant, at least.

The entire space, from floor to walls to low ceiling, was constructed of gleaming, time-burnished wood. In the soft light of the overhead bulb, each crook, cranny, and surface glowed a warm welcome. On the far end of the room, which was ten steps away, if that, the built-in-bed—a nook really— that Maddie had mentioned, was made up with soft white linens, a poufy duvet (also in white), and three plump pillows.

Stevie turned slightly and there, just behind her, beside the door, was the built-in "bureau" Maddie referred to. Stevie was glad to have a name for it because she would've just called it a dresser. The mirror had gold detailing around its edges that caught the light and sparkled.

Maddie waited, expecting a comment of some kind, Stevie guessed—but she couldn't speak. Could only gawk some more, take in yet another detail.

The two walls running between the bureau and bed were not actually "walls" at all. They were floor-to-ceiling shelves. And there was the awesome apple barrel, near the head of the bed, like the most perfect bedside table ever. Stevie closed her eyes for a minute. Yes, Maddie was right. The softest hint of summer ripened apples kissed her senses. She opened her eyes again.

"This is really where you want me to stay while I'm here?"

Maddie gave her a searching look. "Is that all right?"

Stevie's face flamed. "All right? No, it's perfect. So cozy and snug and . . . " She'd been about to add *safe*, but that sounded so lame. "I . . . love it."

"Me too! I could never bring myself to change it or remodel it. The only changes this room has seen since the house was built was that someone installed a light and an electrical socket, long before my husband and me—" Maddie's voice cracked a little on the last word, and Stevie thought she knew how Maddie felt. Grief and missing a person punched extra hard sometimes, usually when you least expected it. "Anyway," Maddie continued after a breath, "I'm especially glad now that I didn't change it. It must've been meant for you all along."

The casual comment did something funny to Stevie's sinuses. She coughed and turned away from Maddie. As lovely a thought as that was—that something good could've been meant for her all along—and as much as she'd enjoyed every minute of her night here at Maddie's house, guilt suddenly soured Stevie's stomach. Wherever Marilyn was, she was definitely not having as nice a time—and whether she did a crap job of it or not, Marilyn was her mother. Wasn't Stevie meant for *her* all along?

"Um, I'm really tired. Can I go to bed now?"

"Of course, honey." Maddie's head tilted as if silently adding, "Are you okay?"

Stevie pretended she didn't notice the silent query, said thanks, and slipped back to the main entrance where her backpack and a small black garbage bag holding all her other belongings sat by her jacket and sneakers.

She had just finished brushing her teeth in the main floor's washroom when there was a light tap on the door.

"No rush at all, but do you need anything before I go up to check on Alissa, Hailey, and Jo?"

Stevie spat into the sink. "No. I'm good. Thanks."

After a moment, Maddie spoke again. "Okay, sweet dreams. See you in the morning."

Stevie carefully rinsed the white ceramic basin, making sure not one speck of toothpaste lingered. She waited until she heard Maddie's footsteps on the stairs, then slung her pack over her shoulder, scooped up the garbage bag, and eased out of the bathroom. Checking both ways, she zipped down the hall, slipped through the dining room, and found the kitchen.

Finally, she was tucked into that little room and burrowing into that crisp, clean nest of a bed. Her sinuses were still full, and her eyes were itchy and hot. She stared up at the inky blackness above her and willed away dark thoughts. Forced herself to imagine, instead, all the kinds of desserts and dishes the person who'd stayed in this room before her might have made with all those apples once stored here.

Stevie stretched in the luxurious bed, loving the smooth cotton against her bare legs and reveling in the scent of coffee wafting to her room and the soft clank of dishes from whoever was already up and puttering in the kitchen. It was one of the best parts of this bedroom, the homey feeling of being included—when she wasn't even in the room yet!

Suddenly her eyes flashed open. It was Christmas morning! She was hit with very conflicting feelings: Excitement. Disappointment. She was thrilled the big day was here. She, Jo, Alissa, Hailey, and Maddie had been looking forward to it so much. The downside to its arrival, however, was a biggie. It meant, no doubt, that her time here would wrap up soon.

The last few days had been a lovely, surreal blur of shopping, baking, playing board games, and visiting with Maddie's mother, Claire. There were so many highlights that Stevie couldn't have picked any particular favorites. No wait, that was a lie. Three things did stand out.

The first occurred when Stevie helped Hailey decorate a sugar cookie, and Hailey had looked up at her with a big grin instead of her usual tentative smile. "I always wanted a big sister with hair like mine."

Her comment made Stevie choke on her cookie. Hailey's hair was a lovely strawberry blond, so soft and shiny and gently curly that she looked like a little angel. Stevie's mop was definitely more carrot than strawberry—but she didn't want to put her low self-esteem on this precious kid, so she just smiled. "I used to daydream about having sisters too."

Her words made everyone go quiet for a second. Then Jo and Alissa both exclaimed, "Me too!" at the same time. The whole table laughed.

The other really special moment wasn't a moment at all; it was a constant so wonderful it made her heart hurt even though she was happy to be a part of it. Stevie was awed by Maddie and Claire, Maddie's mother, and couldn't help but watch them. They were like some really funny, really heartwarming, really educational TV show or something. She didn't have any experience with other adult daughter/mother relationships, and she didn't know if Maddie and Claire were the norm or what, but studying them made her think. She hadn't been enough for her mom obviously, and/or, one could argue, her mom was bad at the whole parenting thing. But in her mom's defense, Marilyn had never had anyone like Claire around to love her either. That was what was so cool about Maddie and Claire. You could see their love for each other, even when they were teasing each other—maybe especially then. For as long as Stevie had been with Marilyn, it was always just the two of them. She couldn't help but wonder. . . . Maybe if Marilyn had someone like Claire in her life, things would have gone really differently than they had. But that was too sad for Christmas.

Stevie popped out of bed and smoothed down the beautiful flannel nightie Maddie had given her the night before. Feeling like a little kid, she bounced into the kitchen to help prep a breakfast feast to enjoy after gift opening.

"Merry Christmas!" Hailey and Alissa yelled the second they entered the room, making her grin.

"Merry Christmas, weirdos," she muttered back—and everyone laughed. It made her feel silly and warm inside. Instead of side eying her, they seemed to totally get her sense of humor.

"Perfect timing!" Maddie announced. "Let's open presents."

Stevie was touched by Hailey's gift: a little notebook with a fox on its front cover. Even more adorable was Hailey's shy whisper, "I thought you'd like it because of your name. Get it?"

"I *do* get it. Good one," Stevie whispered back, "and I love it. Thank you."

Stevie immediately knew what she was going to use it for:

writing out any recipes or cooking instructions Maddie gave her, so she could keep them always.

Jo had gotten her a little gift too: a rechargeable flashlight. The others seemed mildly surprised by the gift, murmuring, "Oh, nice . . ." in a not quite convincing way as if relieved Jo hadn't gotten them flashlights. But Stevie laughed with loud, surprised delight—at the gift, but also at the bubbly glee rising up in her. She and Jo had an inside joke! She'd read about inside jokes before but had never had one. The first thing Jo said when she saw Stevie's wonderful room their first morning was, "It's perfect, but you need a light to read in bed!"

After the last gift was opened, they all galloped back to the kitchen and did the final work toward their Christmas breakfast feast. And that was highlight number three. Stevie loved every minute of being directed by Maddie about how to do this or mix that, and she was beyond thrilled when Maddie asked if she could follow a recipe.

"I think so, yeah," she said—and Maddie got her to make blueberry waffles all by herself! The chore took on even more special significance when she discovered that blueberry waffles for Christmas brunch were part of Maddie and her husband and daughter's holiday tradition.

Later that night, while everybody played with their gifts and visited some more, Stevie replayed the day, recalling each moment in as much detail as possible, wanting to commit it all to memory, so she could pull it out again and again in the future. It wasn't the gifts that made the day so special. It wasn't even the food. It was that she'd never been surrounded by people who were so happy to be together. Even when she was quiet, lost in her thoughts from time to time—or the others were—it felt like they all belonged. And suddenly, just like that, it was too much.

Stevie needed to be alone. She asked Maddie if she could go sit on the porch for a bit.

"Of course. Let me get you a blanket."

Stevie hadn't been outside in the big wicker rocking chair for long when Maddie joined her, two cups of hot chocolate in hand.

"I know the last thing you probably want right now is something else to eat, but I thought hot chocolate out on the porch, surrounded by the crispy snow and the stars above, felt extra Christmassy."

Stevie smiled. It really did.

"Also, I wanted to check in with you. It's been such a wonderful Christmas for me, but it feels bittersweet too. I wondered if it's the same for you."

Stevie nodded. That was the thing about Maddie—why she was so loved not only by her but by all the kids at school. She just . . . got you.

"I don't know." Stevie gestured at the big house behind her, its windows glowing with Christmas lights and shadows of its happy occupants flitting past here and there. "This is all so great, but it also sucks, you know?"

Maddie nodded.

"Part of me feels awful having fun when my mom probably isn't . . . and when, like, I don't know where she is."

"I get that."

"She's not a totally bad person, you know. She's not."

Maddie nodded again. "I know."

"And when you asked if I would like to live with you and I said yes, I meant it. I really did. But I also know it's not possible."

Maddie's head tilted as if Stevie's last comment confused her. She sank onto a bench beside the wicker rocking chair and pulled a piece of Stevie's blanket over her lap.

"What do you mean 'not possible?'"

"Just that, well . . ." For a second, Stevie couldn't find the words, but then she spoke in a rush. "Jo, Alissa, Hailey . . . They don't have moms. They don't have families. They're free to live here with you forever if that's what you all want. But that's not how it is for me."

Maddie looked down and was uncharacteristically quiet for a long time.

Here it comes, thought Stevie. I'm right. My mom's already shown up again, or Natalie's told Maddie I have to go back to a group home or something because I have a parent. Maddie probably just wanted to spare me the bad news until after Christmas because, of course, she's nice like that.

Finally, Maddie spoke. "When I asked if you wanted to live with me, Stevie, I wasn't just asking out the blue. I'd already asked Natalie how it would work and if it would be possible—not because I care whether the arrangements will be difficult—no matter how difficult they are, I'll see them through—but because I didn't want to disappoint you again. You've already had enough disappointments for a whole life-time, and then some."

Stevie tucked her half of the blanket around herself a little more tightly and waited for it. "But?" she asked.

"No buts. For as long as your mom is not here, this is your home. And if, *when*, your mom shows up again, we'll take it from there. If you need—or want—to live with her again, I want you to know you'll always have a home here with me too."

"Really?" It sounded to Stevie like Maddie was saying that she was going to be there for her from here on out, no matter what—that it didn't matter what the details were. Everything would just be okay. Maddie would always watch out for her.

She hadn't realized she'd expressed that thought aloud until Maddie squeezed her shoulder and said, "Yes, that's exactly what I mean. You got it."

Stevie had watched a lot of Christmas specials on TV. She'd sang Christmas carols and heard a zillion of them on the radio. She'd read countless books containing Christmas "themes" as Mr. B. would say, but until that moment, she'd never understood how truly merry and perfect—and life-changing—a Christmas really could be.

"I'm . . . I'm just going to sit out here a little while longer," Stevie said.

"You bet. Take all the time you need." Maddie got to her feet—and was almost at the door when Stevie whispered, "Maddie?"

"Yeah?"

Stevie swallowed against the hard lump in her throat. "Thank you," she whispered.

"Aw, sweetie . . . you're so welcome. Merry Christmas."

CHAPTER 1

FIFTEEN YEARS LATER

S tevie glared at the most recent text message then jabbed her phone with angry thumbs. She was aware even as she responded that the fury flooding through her was merely a cover for the wave of deep, desperate sadness threatening to drown her. "Are you sure?" she typed.

A response came immediately. Three frowning faces and one word. "Absolutely."

Then. "I'm sorry."

Stevie's stomach churned. Her sister Jo was the most level-headed, loyal, dependable person Stevie had ever known except for their adoptive mom, Maddie. She would never in a million years lie or stretch the truth or tease about something like . . . this. "Have to go," she finally typed. "Will msg soon."

No reply, but Stevie hadn't expected one. She set her phone down on her RV's little dinette table, and for the first time ever, its vintage laminate surface—cream with gold stars —failed to cheer her.

She pressed her clenched fists into her tightly closed eyes, hard. "Do not cry," she muttered. "*Do. Not.*"

She forced some deep breaths—hard work over the

choking lump in her throat—then slowly, resolutely got back to her feet.

People always asked what her glitch was. Why she was so jaded. Well, this was why. This was what hoping got you. This was what trusting did.

Jed was supposed to be one of the good guys. He'd gotten past her defenses. Gotten past all their defenses.

She pivoted and took one step to reach the custom-built chest freezer with its lid that did double duty as counter space when she needed to roll out dough. Opening the freezer, which held very little except for one precious thing taking up almost all the room, Stevie's eyes swam despite her iron resolve.

Looking down, it was like the fondant creation of doves and ribbons mocked her. She lifted the cake out and moved to the RV's door. It was slightly ajar because she'd been airing the RV after simmering three different sauces all morning. Kicking the door open with one foot, she lifted the cake high above her head, then heaved it forward.

It dropped heavily and smashed open on the frozen snow-packed earth. Destroyed layers of decadent chocolate and soft vanilla cream revealed a sweet, delicate fruit and custard center. A murder of crows—what an appropriate name, Stevie thought, darkly amused—scattered in shock from their perch in the barren arms of a nearby tree, then settled on the ground close by and hopped over to feast.

Nowhere near finished, Stevie went back to her tiny design marvel of a kitchen and opened a cupboard to pull out the "surprise." Easing the box top off, she stared down at Jed and, more importantly, Alissa—in perfect miniature detail. Taking in her little sister's beaming heart-shaped face, with her wide brown eyes and pretty bobbed hair—so open, so trusting, so deserving of so much better than . . . *Jed*, Stevie's breathing was once more threatened by burning outrage and tears she wouldn't let escape.

A tiny bride and groom smiled up, hands clasped, and arms lifted in joy and victory. They were an exact replica of Alissa and Jed, created by a genius cake topper designer from photos Stevie had taken when they'd announced their engagement.

Stevie reached forward, about to grab Jed by the neck—but suddenly couldn't follow through. What if she accidentally damaged mini Alissa somehow? Even if Alissa didn't know this item existed, Stevie couldn't bear hurting her even by accident, effigy or not. She resealed the box, slid it back into the cupboard, then did the next best thing.

She rummaged for the generic cake topper—Plan B, purchased in case the special order didn't turn out or arrive in time. Grabbing her sharpest paring knife and a cutting board, she plunged the blade through Jed's plastic core. How apt. He'd fooled everyone into thinking his heart—and affections —were real.

She snapped pictures of the impaled groom, withdrew her knife, and strode to the doorway. Throwing Jed onto the wrecked cake, she took a few more photos. The majority of the crows flapped off in a tizzy of black wings, cawing and shrieking in annoyance. Two crows weren't scared off by the falling groom, however, and continued to greedily devour the cake around him. They were a particularly good, if macabre, addition to the photos.

She would never show these pics to poor Alissa, of course. But Jed? She'd send them to him, all right—with the wish she could land a hard punch to somewhere tender at the same time.

"How could you?" she typed. "Alissa is worth a billion of you. You . . ." Stevie had no more words, but that didn't matter. Actions spoke more honestly and clearly than any of the most eloquent speeches. Jed would get her point. She hit send. Then went to each picture and hit send and send again.

Finally, still buzzing with stress, she replied to Jo again, as promised. First, with the pictures.

To which she received a flurry of texts, including one that said, "Do not, under any circumstances, send those to Alissa, or Hailey, or Mom."

"Of course not. Unlike Jed, I'm not a callous idiot or worse."

Before Jo could agree or disagree with that statement, Stevie got to the real guts of the matter. "What are we going to do? What does Alissa need?"

CHAPTER 2

Waiting for Jo to reply with a concrete plan, Stevie spent some time beating herself up and second-guessing her recent choices. If only she was parked and living in their hometown Granite Ridge right now, the way she so often was. Instead, she was just returning from an extended season cooking at a fishing lodge in British Columbia. When the wedding was on, meeting up with everyone at the venue instead of going to Granite Ridge first made sense and saved her some travel hours. Now she wished she'd done everything differently. If she was in town, she would've shown up at her mom's house to help out.

She could, of course, call her mom or Hailey to get instructions about what to do next herself, instead of depending on Jo for guidance, but she didn't want to distract them from helping Alissa in whatever ways they could.

Pacing her RV's narrow space, Stevie perused the photos she'd taken of the demolished wedding cake. Her response to the news that Jed had broken up with Alissa and called off their Christmas Eve wedding was justified. Yet reviewing the destruction of that iconic symbol of love and hope for the future didn't give her any satisfaction. If anything, it made her feel worse. She prayed awful Jed wouldn't message Alissa about the cake and his murdered mini-him. It would only make kind, tender-hearted Alissa even sadder.

Dang it! Why hadn't Jo messaged back already? What was keeping her? Not being able to do something, anything, was maddening. Unconsciously, Stevie glanced toward Ed's bed, which she hadn't been able to bring herself to part with yet. If he was still around, at least she'd have him to talk to or take for a walk or something to get her mind off . . . everything.

With that thought, the tears Stevie had been fighting since Jo's first text earlier that afternoon won. She cried silently, her body rigid and still. It was something she'd learned how to do too many years ago to count: let her emotions escape without a telltale sound or movement. No one who happened to walk past her home on wheels and glance in the window would know she was sobbing.

Some of her tears were for herself. She had to be honest and admit that even if it showed what a selfish jerk she was. She couldn't help it. Alissa and Jed had been a couple who'd given her hope that good guys existed, and love could be real. Proof that no matter how crappy your background was, you could rise above it.

Most of her tears were genuinely for Alissa though, triggered by deep sorrow for what her sister must be feeling, frustration at being powerless to fix anything for her, and worry. Stevie knew Alissa had all the grit she needed and then some to get through this. She just hoped Alissa could see past her pain and know it as well.

It wasn't fair. Little Alissa had already gone through enough loss for a lifetime. *Little Alissa.* Stevie almost smiled, seeing the eye roll Alissa would give if she'd heard that thought. But she couldn't help thinking of her that way. Even though her sister was twenty-five-years-old now and a certified teacher to boot, she was somehow still the innocent, no-idea-how-great-she-was kid Stevie had first met all those years ago, when Alissa was ten and Stevie, thirteen. Just like how Hailey was perpetually eight in Stevie's mind, and Jo would always be a super cool fifteen to her awkward, lame thirteen. It was weird with siblings how that happened, you all grew up—or mostly did, Stevie thought, making a face at herself. Yet, you all stayed kids around each other too in that way siblings do, for better or worse.

Alissa struggled with abandonment and self-worth issues like they all did in various ways. No matter how much you grow as a person or strive to work through them, some things are so deeply formative that even when you no longer let them define you, they're forever a shadow side of you, shaping your view of the world and your place in it. With her deep fear of loss, letting herself love Jed had been a big deal. That he knew Alissa lost her parents and bounced around from home to home before she arrived at Maddie's, yet still took all her trust and selfless, generous care, and promised her *forever*, only to reject her and throw it back in Alissa's face? Well, as the cake and plastic groom incident might've hinted, it made Stevie want to—

Her phone buzzed, and she snatched it up with relief. Too much time in her head was never good. She read Jo's text and replied. "You got it. I'll be there."

Another message popped back almost immediately. "I'm so sad about the change in circumstances surrounding our visit, but at least our whole family's going to be together again. I can't wait to see you!"

Stevie didn't waste time wondering if going up to Cedar Mountain Lodge as originally planned was a good idea or a terrible one. If that's what Alissa wanted and needed, to make what was supposed to be a celebratory getaway into a journey of mourning and saying goodbye—and hopefully a cathartic, healing time with her sisters—she and the rest of her sisters, her *family*, would make it so.

She closed her eyes briefly. Even though this Christmas

marked the fifteenth anniversary of Maddie bringing them together, the miracle of it never lost its shine. No matter what else happened in her life, no matter how she'd probably never scrounge up the courage to take a romantic risk herself—regardless of how she sometimes dreamed of a husband and children to love and take care of—she had this. Had *them*: Jo, Hailey, Alissa, Maddie, and Maddie's mom, Nan Claire. It was the kind of thing Stevie always imagined as a lonely kid, nose constantly in a library book, waiting on her mom who so seldom—then never—came home. Imagined, but never dreamed actually *possible*. She was blessed in so many ways, and she knew all too well that the nuclear family she sometimes fantasized about and yearned for was often just that: a fantasy. That the reality of family was, if you could forgive the pun, all too often *nuclear*. What you loved could blow up and be lost forever, damaging you irreparably. It was exactly why she didn't want to take chances or rock the boat she'd found herself in.

She shook her arms, then stretched, eyes wide open again. All this lollygagging wouldn't do. There was a plan now! She had to get her butt in gear. Lists of all that needed to be done before she hit the road in the morning filled her head, but most importantly—

"Exactly how I feel, Jo!" she typed and sent.

Then, wracking her brain for something, anything, she could say to Alissa that might be of comfort or cheer—and feeling extra terrible when she came up empty because Alissa, like Hailey, was a words girl—she settled with sending a string of heart emoticons, the promise she'd see her the next day as originally scheduled, and the suggestion, "We can spend the week planning his slow and painful death." She nodded with satisfaction once the last bit was sent. Maddie would be level-headed and eternally supportive. Jo would be logical and comforting. Alissa would be all heart. Stevie would rein in her rage the best she could, but someone, she thought, should let Alissa know revenge was an option. She was only half-joking.

But now, Stevie had food to make. She'd lived through puberty, first crushes, date disasters, and tons of other silly, serious, and sublime moments with Alissa. "Crazy comforting cheesy mac"—so named by Alissa when she was sixteen or so and doing remedial work one summer so she wouldn't be held back in school—was definitely on the menu.

The mountains and trees hugging the highway were blanketed in white, and while the roads were in decent shape, fresh snow was falling. Stevie hoped it would let up before Maddie and Nan started their drive up.

Turning into Cedar Mountain Lodge's huge parking area and following the signs toward a designated area for overnight parking, Stevie couldn't help gawking. Even though the next weeks would no doubt be excruciating in a lot of ways, the surrounding scenery was magical. So pretty it almost hurt. Towering cedars draped in white robes stretched into a gorgeous purple-blue sky. The ancient mountain ranges formed a protective bowl around the magnificent lodge and surrounding ski village, which were lit up with a dazzling array of Christmas lights and twinkled like Santa's workshop. And the snow! The snow! It sparkled in the bright winter sun like a blanket of diamonds as far as the eye could see, a white so clean and pristine it was almost startling.

Stevie pulled to a stop at a gate and lowered her window to show the attendant her ID and the reservation number on her phone.

The guy, big and bearded, looked about her age and had a friendly smile. "I haven't seen your rig before. Work or play?"

Stevie grinned. She'd expected some variation of a similar question. No doubt, many of the folks camped up here were seasonal workers who moved around the country, working at this lodge or another, as she often did.

"No, it's my little sister's wedding—" The words died on her tongue. What an idiot she was! What if she made an insensitive slip like that in front of Alissa? "I'm here to, I mean *as*, a guest," she finished haltingly after an awkward beat.

The man looked curious at her weird delivery but shrugged. "Well . . . enjoy yourself, all right?"

Stevie nodded, then eased toward the spot where she'd been directed. The sites had full service. Bonus. Her vintage motorhome—1986 Toyota Sunraders for the win, baby!—was set up for off-grid living and had a generator. Considering the nightmare the next twelve days were likely to be, it was a relief that she could just plug in and be set.

Before she got out of her vehicle, she leaned forward and rested her forehead on the steering wheel. Seeing Alissa heartbroken and not being able to do a darn thing about it was going to do her in. She wasn't like her sisters. She had none of Jo's deep, calming competence. None of Alissa's sweetness or gentle, naturally soothing demeanor. Not a drop of Hailey's uncanny ability to read people in a glance and know intuitively exactly what they needed.

As always, no matter how she tried to fight it, when thinking about all her inadequacies, especially in light of her talented, brilliant, warm, and sensitive sisters, icy fingers of fear and self-loathing poked tender inner bruises. One day they'd realize that all the strengths they insisted she had were merely projections from their overly kind hearts—qualities they wished for her, not any that she actually possessed. And then they wouldn't love her anymore. Maddie still would—because she was a softie for a lost cause, obviously.

For a moment, the temptation to restart the motorhome's engine and retreat the way she'd come almost overpowered her.

The worst part of her desire to bail was that her stupid, lovable sisters would be so understanding if she did. Alissa would muster a smile, despite her grief, and say she totally "got it." Jo would sigh resignedly—but with sympathy—and say Stevie should do whatever she needed for her own mental health. And it wouldn't just be passive-aggressive bullshit. She'd actually mean it. Hailey, ever the peacemaker, would nod at whatever Jo and Alissa said, then step up her game and help Alissa in every possible way, always trying to make up for other people's failings.

Maddie would encourage her to reconsider—but would ultimately affirm Stevie's choice and tell her she'd love and support her no matter what.

Stevie banged her forehead lightly against the steering wheel. Running the minute something was hard—or heck, just not fun—was something her mother would do. She was not her mother's daughter! Or she was, but she was also *Maddie's*. She was Maddie's daughter too. She *was*.

And if Maddie had taught Stevie anything, it was that the only real way forward in hard times was to help others and focus on trying to be the good in the world. It was hard to imagine someone as inconsequential as herself having any real power, but still . . . she would persevere, do what she could, and hope it was enough.

Not necessarily feeling better, but definitely feeling resolved again, Stevie climbed out of her home, plugged it in, and turned the stove, heater, and pump on inside. Then filling a bag to bursting with goodies for Alissa—but keeping the Christmas presents she had for everyone else stashed where they were, so they'd be secrets until the big day, or quiet day, maybe—she set off to find her sisters. They should all be there by now.

CHAPTER 3

E ven though it was a relief for Stevie to be with her sisters again, to see that they were fine and that no one had disappeared or become unalterably changed in her absence, dinner was a sad affair. So sad, in fact, that she felt bad for the wait staff.

The handsome guy serving them had, understandably, thought four young women dining at a place like Cedar Mountain Lodge would mean a festive mood, friendly flirting, quite-possibly tipsy laughter from their end. He realized his mistake with shame-faced speed and quickly matched their somber tone. While his service remained impeccable, he assumed an almost embarrassed air around them.

If only Maddie was there. Her soothing presence would've made things much better straightaway. As it was, the way everyone picked at their meals, herself being the only exception—she practically inhaled the seafood pie she'd ordered—they probably should've stayed in Alissa's suite and just shared the cheesy mac Stevie had brought for her. However, none of them had wanted to gobble up Alissa's "treat." Although Alissa had been her gracious self when she accepted the abundance of comfort food Stevie had made for her (the pasta being only the start) and put it into her room's mini-fridge, Stevie was kicking herself. She'd brought a ton of food. *Food*! Yes, it was a great solace in hard times and maybe the best way of bringing people together in good times . . . but in light of what Alissa was suffering, it was meaningless. She wished she could do . . . more. Just always. *More*.

It was still early when they finished eating, and Hailey asked if anyone was interested in going for drinks at Granite Bar. Jo and Alissa begged off, but Stevie, who would've been happiest if they all gathered in her RV or in someone's room to chat into the wee hours, quickly agreed. She'd take sister time, whatever it looked like.

As she and Hailey got their coats on, Jo apologized one more time for being too tired to visit longer. Stevie just laughed. "We're getting old, hey?"

"Oh, yeah, *ancient*."

"Wait, one more thing," Stevie said before Jo made her getaway.

Jo smiled and raised an eyebrow. "What's that?"

"Still work for me to use your bathroom every so often?" Stevie had asked to take advantage of Jo's full-size shower and tub at the lodge before—but prior to the whole Jed dumping Alissa debacle. It would be totally understandable if it was the last thing on Jo's mind, but Stevie hoped it would still be a go. It was the only part of RV living that occasionally got old. Her shower "stall" was incredibly narrow even for a dwarf like her, and the "tub" it sprayed into was really a small basin, only suitable for standing in.

"Absolutely. Any time."

Stevie watched her stylish older sister depart, looking every inch the sophisticated lawyer she was, even in her casual outfit of well-cut jeans, a fitted sweater, and gorgeous boots. She glanced down at her own "signature" winter outfit —a gray hoodie and yoga pants. The only way it varied from her spring, summer, and fall look is that she sometimes sported a long-sleeve T-shirt instead of a tank top or wore jeans if she was feeling really dressy. What could she say? She liked to be comfortable and favored clothes you could work in for hours. Plus, there was the added bonus that clothes like this made you virtually invisible. With her hair scraped back in a messy topknot or tight ponytail and in her always clean but nondescript garb, no one gave her a second glance. Precisely what she preferred.

Granite Bar was crowded and loud, with a great band and delicious scents wafting from the kitchen. She was tempted to check out their menu, despite having just eaten. It was the kind of place Stevie would've usually enjoyed to the hilt. Now, however, though she'd been ecstatic that Hailey wanted to hang out, she realized she wasn't in the mood for a party atmosphere. They chatted over a drink and caught up, both more than a little blue about Alissa's situation.

A guy from the band named Nick, who Stevie knew from high school, wandered over to say hi. He expressed obvious interest in Hailey, who equally obviously returned it. Stevie had to smile at Hailey's slightly starstruck expression—even while she felt more than a little shocked. How could Hailey think of romance when how badly relationships always went was so crystal clear at the moment?

Increasingly twitchy and desperately in need of a walk to burn off energy, after Hailey and Nick had danced a few times, Stevie asked if Hailey was ready to head out.

Hailey darted a glance toward Nick, and Stevie caught the look.

Normally, Stevie would never leave one of her sisters alone at a bar. Still, Nick was a known quantity—and a genuinely good guy—so when Hailey insisted Stevie go ahead without her, she did.

The rush of cold air, silence, and bright stars overhead that greeted Stevie as she emerged from the bar were a relief, but she knew without a sprinkle of doubt that sleep was hours and hours away. Usually, that wouldn't bother her in the slightest, but these days all the solitude she enjoyed wasn't as satisfying somehow. She shook her head. No doubt, the annoying itch of weird longing for something she couldn't quite articulate (or didn't want to, more like it!) was just a side effect of her sadness over losing Ed. Without him to curl up beside and read with, the call of her snug little home on wheels was less appealing than usual. She nodded to herself. Yes, that was it—and that was all it was.

She'd hoped that being clear of the bar's hyper energy would mellow her out, but nope. She was still antsy and decided that the walk she'd mentioned to Hailey was still on the menu. Definitely. She'd explore the lodge grounds and surrounding ski village and hopefully burn off some of her anxious energy.

As she started out, she was shocked by the temperature difference from when she'd arrived that afternoon and now. The sun hadn't felt warm, but now that it was dark, it was obvious it had been giving off some heat, after all. She loosened her hair and let it fall around her shoulders to keep the back of her neck warmer. Then she buttoned up the wool pea coat she'd thrown on over her sweatshirt before leaving the RV for dinner. The pretty moss green jacket was too light a weight for this weather—or so she now knew, anyway—but it had been a gift from Maddie. She wanted her family to see her wearing it, so they'd know she appreciated it.

Kitty-corner from the lodge's main entrance, soft music tinkled from a bar with an old-fashioned sign that announced, "Jackson's Public House." Warm yellow light shone onto the snow from its slightly steamy mullioned windows. Drawn by the cozy image, Stevie crossed the street and meandered toward it, sticking to the well-shoveled sidewalk that fronted a little row of specialty shops. Each was closed up and dark inside, but their exteriors were aglow with Christmas bulbs. Her breath formed huge feathery plumes of white in the night air, and—whew, it was brisk.

She decided that despite how pretty the night was, she wouldn't venture about for much longer—would only go as far as Jackson's front entrance to see if there was a menu posted by the door. She was curious about whether the quaint looking establishment actually offered good old school pub fare. She'd barely reached the rear corner of the building, however, when a sudden commotion stopped her in her tracks.

A big metal door—invisible until it slammed open and bright white kitchen light spilled across the dark courtyard— crashed against the pub's brick exterior. A woman blasted out. Throwing off an apron and swearing a blue streak, she stormed past Stevie like she wasn't even there.

An equally irate man in a black chef's coat appeared in the doorway. Backlit by the fluorescent light pouring from behind him, his features were invisible in the darkness. He was like a furious shadow as he yelled, "Don't bother to come back when you're 'sorry.' You're done!"

He took a few angry strides after the woman as if despite his big words, he already regretted her departure. The woman was long gone, though—and since she hadn't been wearing a coat, Stevie understood her speed.

The man, evidently as oblivious to Stevie's presence as the woman had been, raged into the night, "Are you freaking kidding me?"

Stevie smiled to herself. It was hard not to sympathize with a guy who, at the height of anger, used "freaking" as his curse word of choice.

The man locked his hands against the back of his head and stared out into the empty night, his bent elbows like rigid wings on either side of his face. Weirdly, there was something familiar about this position and his body language in general.

After a long minute, he dropped his clenched hands

abruptly, and his shoulders sagged. "What am I going to do now?" he muttered.

Come to think about it, even the guy's voice rang a bell.

"*What*?" he snapped, turning toward her like she'd said something—which she hadn't. So maybe he'd seen her all along, had just been too preoccupied to acknowledge her. "Unless you're trained kitchen help, bugger off."

Knowing from personal experience that most cooks are at least partially mad, Stevie wasn't put off by the rudeness. Had she worked with him somewhere before? If yes, it had to have been a good while back.

"That's exactly what I am, actually." She stepped out of the shadows and stuck her hand out, about to introduce herself—because, hey, connections in the culinary world were always good—just as he moved back into the full light streaming from the kitchen. And then they both went rigid with surprise.

What the— Now she wanted to be the one who swore! Was this some terrible cosmic joke?

He looked as face-punched as she felt—which made no sense. She, after all, was the injured party all those years ago.

"Stevie . . . Fox?" The voice that had seemed so familiar was now a dry, shocked croak.

She didn't see how she could believably deny it. "*Jackson Basset*," she replied. "What are the chances?"

CHAPTER 4

Now that Jackson—*Jackson!*—was standing in the light, Stevie couldn't believe she hadn't recognized him instantly from his silhouette and body language, let alone his voice. He'd put on man muscle, was a little thicker than his teenage self, and his voice was deeper— or maybe only because it was so angry. Yet, the more she stared, the more identical he seemed—and the more bizarre it was that she hadn't recognized him. He was scarred into her psyche. How had she not known it was him right off? She'd have thought her body would've had the decency to cue her in, at least.

Her skin should've crawled. Or the hair on the back of her neck could have prickled. Her hackles might've raised. Did humans even have hackles? No matter. It was beside the point because, as she'd already established, her body had failed to warn her. Worse, her traitorous brain, instead of shoring up her defenses and preparing to go on the offensive if needed, was pointing out that he was still really good look- ing, maybe even more good looking than he'd been in high school, actually. Because that was a super helpful thing to focus on. Thanks, brain.

Jackson pulled off the bandana he'd been wearing to hold his hair back while cooking and shook his head as if in disbelief. His hair was still the same, too—a tumble of silky black waves that fell almost to his shoulders.

"It never even occurred to me that you might still be around here." He shook his head again. "How long has it been since we last saw each other?"

Of course, he wouldn't remember! Okay, it's not like she knew the exact date herself or anything, but still. Stevie crossed her arms over her chest. He'd been privy to the most painful years of her life and added to the humiliating hell of it. What did it matter if either of them remembered the last incident or not?

Apparently, he didn't need or expect a real answer because he started to ask if she'd stayed in the area the whole time since graduation and if Maddie still had that "cool" house—then changed gears, sounding surprised. "If looks could kill. What on earth are you glaring at me for?"

"Maybe I just don't want to go down memory lane with you. Not everyone thinks you're as awesome as you do."

"Wow." The bitterness in Jackson's voice surprised Stevie so much that she took a step back. It was like she'd touched a nerve—which was impossible. Jackson Basset didn't have nerves. "Glad to see some things never change. You're still the same old Stevie—in other words, crazy."

The comment hurt a little. It was too close to the mark. She did act kind of crazy around Jackson, always had. She couldn't help it. In school, he'd been everything she wanted and knew she'd never have. She shoved her coat sleeves up to her elbows, then frowned. The gesture was a tell, something she always did when she was overwrought. She hoped Jackson didn't recognize—or remember it—as such.

"If this is how you talk to anyone who volunteers to help you, no wonder they leave. Maybe you should take a clue. It's not them. It's you."

Jackson didn't appear to hear her. Instead, he leaned in, took her wrist, and held her arm up toward the light. Stevie was so shocked by the feeling of his warm fingers on her always-cold flesh that she didn't jerk away immediately—and then she realized what he was so focused on. She was practically blind to it by now, but it always drew other people's eye: a thick, shiny scar—still an angry red—on the inside of her forearm about two inches from the hollow of her elbow joint.

Jackson traced the shiny mark with one finger, and Stevie was hit by an unhappy—yet simultaneously treasured—memory of how tactile he was. How physical.

"This is a kitchen scar. The kind you get pulling trays from an oven in a hurry and accidentally touching your flesh to the rack above."

"Yeah, and?" Stevie couldn't keep the *so what* note out of her voice.

"You mean you actually kept cooking? You have legit restaurant experience?"

Stevie stared at him. "Of course, I do. Why would I tell you I did if I didn't? Who would lie about something like this?"

Jackson shrugged. "You'd be surprised what people will do to get close to my dad's money. Before I realized you were . . . you, I thought maybe you knew my family and were angling to—"

"Oh, that's right!" Stevie cut him off as another rush of Jackson-centered high school memories surfaced again. She had done so much to tamp them down that she was surprised all the details were still so . . . available. Especially this one, which was the least compelling element of Jackson Basset's many qualities. "I forgot. You're Richie Rich."

Jackson started to scowl, then let out a low laugh instead. "And I always forgot, you were the one person my money never impressed. So . . . " He shot a glance back toward the kitchen door and looked at her again, suddenly sheepish. "I really am in a bind. Will you forgive me for being a jerk and help me out tonight?"

Was he asking her to forgive him for being a jerk now or all those years ago? She studied his face, then glanced at the still-gaping kitchen door, pouring light into the snowy night and emitting the most drool-worthy scent of roasting meat and rich gravy. *Right*. In the shock of meeting him again after all these years, Stevie had almost forgotten the triggering event: he was supposed to be cooking. It felt like they'd been out there forever, but really all the drama and their awkward reunion had taken what, three minutes?

"Fine, but I want the previous woman's hourly wage, plus my choice of the menu for dinner after we close."

A hard to read expression creased Jackson's face, and he scrubbed his stubbled chin as if thinking about a counteroffer. Finally, he stuck out his hand. "Deal."

CHAPTER 5

S tevie hung her jacket on a hook in a closet-sized space with three chairs and table shoved against one wall, generously called the "staff room" by Jackson. Then she donned the apron he passed her after apologizing for not having any extra whites. Last, she scraped her hair back into the elastic she'd removed less than half an hour earlier.

He'd been rushing through a quick intro to where things were in his kitchen but stopped mid-sentence, apparently arrested by the act of her putting her hair into a coiled lump on the nape of her neck.

She raised an eyebrow.

He shrugged. "It's a shame, Fox, that's all."

Stevie burned at his old use of "fox." How she'd hated his mocking use of her last name. She knew full well she was more mouse than fox, and she didn't appreciate the note of obviously insincere innuendo he always put into her name.

"What is?"

Jackson motioned at her hair. "That you have to pull it back. It's so beautiful down."

She glared and scrubbed her hands in the sink designated for such things with a clear label.

"What on earth did I say now?"

As if he didn't know. The problem was he sounded so genuine, just the way he had when they were kids, and she was so dumb. The tiniest part of her always wondered—or wished, more like it—what if he was sincere?

"I said I'd help you for my own reasons. I need to keep busy—but I'm not that teenage kid who will take your bullshit anymore. If you mock me, I'll walk."

She finished washing and drying her hands, then put on gloves from the box by the sink. Jackson was staring at her, eyes slightly narrowed, jaw tight, when she turned around.

"What? This is . . . you are . . ." He started, then stalled. "We're going to talk about what you just said, but not now."

A swinging door banged open beyond Stevie's line of sight, blocked by a huge walk-in cooler. Sounds rushed in: Destiny Child's "8 Days of Christmas" blaring on the sound system, the cheery, booze-enhanced laughter and chat of patrons, and the clatter and rattle of food going out and dirty dishes coming into the pit.

It was all so familiar that Stevie's heart squeezed, and, pathetically, she was instantly sure-footed again.

"Jackson? Val?" The female voice was urgent and slightly annoyed like it wasn't the first time she'd popped into the kitchen to call Jackson and whoever the Val person was— Stevie assumed it was the freshly departed cook's helper or sous chef or whatever this job called the position. "Where are you guys? Six is still waiting on appies. Four wants to know how long their mains are going to be, and Kelly's sat a table of twelve who only came in because our kitchen's still open—"

"On it, Melody," Jackson called back. He gave his hands, which he'd washed too, a vigorous shake, dried them roughly with a paper towel, and grabbed gloves.

He strode in the direction the voice had come from but spoke over his shoulder to Stevie. "It's just pub food, pretty simple fare for the most part—but since you're coming in cold, maybe you can just handle the fryer, any pizza orders, and nachos?"

"Absolutely."

He quickly directed her to the fryer station, showed her the dedicated pizza and nachos oven, and rustled up a menu for her. It was kind of funny that he called where she was working a "station" because it was just the back wall of the kitchen, while he worked nearer the front, with a ten-burner gas stove with dual ovens, a warmer, and a massive grill.

Time sped by—and although Stevie was an old hand at impromptu kitchen work, even she was shocked by how well they worked together. She supposed it helped—in this one instance only—that she was as physically aware of him as ever. He didn't need to say "Behind you" or give any other cue when he crossed her path or moved in her orbit. And vice-versa. By the time 10:30 rolled around, she didn't even need to ask for quantity directions.

If she asked, "Chicken fingers?" or the like, she remembered whatever number she got back in reply. And, conveniently, whoever had created the menu was naturally descriptive. She could recreate most of the things she was required to make from the descriptions therein. "The works" nachos, for example, conveniently listed every topping. Ditto, the evocatively named "haystack eggs," for which she did the potatoes and Jackson did everything else on the grill, and "Volcano fries."

"You're like a fast-food savant," he muttered with what sounded like genuine appreciation at one point. The comment made her laugh—and then blush because he seemed so pleased by her laughter.

At 11:00, there was a lull, and Jackson introduced her to the dish guy, Bernie—who expressed surprise that it was her "first day" because she "seemed so pro." She acknowledged the compliment with a smile and didn't bother to inform him it was her last day too. She started emptying the stainless-steel topping bins and putting food away, following Jackson's lead. At 11:15, Murphy's Law, there was a last call rush for jalapeño poppers and the like.

At 11:30, the kitchen was officially closed, but the pub would stay open later—though probably not much later, Jackson informed her as he filled a marked bucket with a solution of hot water, bleach, and dish detergent.

"Our permit says we can serve until 2:00, but we typically shut down earlier even though it's a holiday destination. Folks are up early to ski or for spa treatments and other similarly grueling activities."

She chuckled again, then teased—but was genuinely curious. "And speaking of grueling 'activities,' what were you busy with while I did all the work?"

It really was a joke. He'd been busier than her, but she was curious about what he'd been cooking and serving up. Whatever it was, it wasn't on the menu she'd been working from—not that what she made was bad. Not at all. It was real food, prepped and cooked in house, from real ingredients—pizza dough made from scratch, hand-cut potatoes for fries, gravy built from actual drippings, not a base, etc. Family, friends, and corporate groups who ate here would enjoy genuinely good food. Even a simple snack would be memorable. Jackson and his staff weren't just opening up plastic bags and reheating prefab food. Yet, at the same time, as he'd said earlier, it was "pretty standard pub fare"—and what he'd been serving, from the quick glimpses she got, was anything but.

He chuckled and looked self-conscious—and Stevie was struck by a huge gaffe on her part. She'd kept inwardly marveling at how much he hadn't changed, how he was exactly the same—except this grown man version of Jackson seemed humble, not perpetually self-assured and confident.

They'd both been busy wrapping food and putting things

away and wiping down surfaces, but now Jackson paused and gestured toward the fryer. "This is all good and fine, but it's not what I'm really into. It just keeps the doors open, you know?"

She did know. Pub fare like she'd been cooking had a relatively good profit margin—and people downed it like there was no tomorrow when they were drinking.

"I offer a five-item du jour menu too—though I admit a couple dishes are so popular, they're almost mainstays these days." He tossed the rag he'd been using into the bleach bucket and withdrew a folded sheet of paper from his pocket. It was divided into an eight-block grid, and handwritten lists filled each one. She scanned the contents of the first four blocks. Each had a big checkmark showing them complete. Then she read the offerings under the underlined heading "19." Her stomach literally rumbled, and her gaze shot up to Jackson's.

"Every single thing sounds . . . amazing. Exactly my cup of tea—and favorite types of things to cook *and* eat."

"Well, that's high praise. Thank you very—" Jackson trailed off and gave Stevie a searching look. "Wait—are you being sarcastic?"

"What? *No*." She gave a little laugh. "I love all food, but what I call "real" food, the kind of stuff people feed their families with, cook for a crowd . . . that's always my favorite."

Jackson's dark eyes were so warm, so transparently happy at her words, like he was flattered or something—as if her opinion actually mattered to him, yeah right!—that Stevie's heart clenched a little. She always remembered that he had gorgeous eyes, of course, but she'd forgotten how expressive they were.

The smile creasing his eyes and lifting the corners of his lush month—not that she'd been staring at it or anything—was replaced by a contemplative expression. "Hopefully, other people share your opinion. This is my last year here.

The building's been sold, and the new owner has something else in mind for this spot."

Before she could ask him what plans, if any, he had for after that happened, he changed gears, letting out a gusty exhale. "I don't know about you, but I'm starved—and I think our work arrangement involved a meal?"

Stevie grinned. She was hungry, but after deep frying all evening and thinking that's what would be offered—something fried—she'd been planning to snack back at her RV, instead. Now she waved the du jour menu she still held. "The mini roast beef stuffed Yorkshire puddings, if you please, sir."

Jackson winked. "Oh, I do please. Definitely."

She bit her lip and shook her head. Part of her wanted to grin; part of her was sixteen again and couldn't bear him taunting her like this.

They ate at a massive table that was sectioned off from the rest of the restaurant by a lattice screen, and Jackson mentioned it was sort of an unofficial staff table. The night was winding down, but there were still a few diehards, drinking and visiting with increasing volume, and the two pool tables were in constant use.

The food was beyond delicious—Stevie savored each bite —and the conversation was fun and light, mostly about kitchen mishaps and nightmare customers. Servers working the floor sat down to listen and chime in now and again, too, as their nights simmered down. As always, Stevie was struck by how restaurant life took on a family life feel.

When Jackson cleared their plates away, then returned with cash in his hand, Stevie was momentarily confused. It had been such a surprisingly fun windup to the night that she'd almost forgotten why they were sharing the meal in the first place.

She laughed and waved away the payment. "I should pay you. This was the perfect way to take my mind of things."

"What things are those?" Jackson sounded concerned.

Stevie hesitated, then relayed Alissa's tale of woe in very brief detail. "Suffice it to say," she finished. "I don't want your money." She grinned. "We'll just agree you owe me."

Jackson's mouth quirked in that sexy, familiar-as-if-she'd-seen-it-yesterday way of his. "Works for me, but don't forget my debt. I really want you to collect."

A rush of heat flooded Stevie's face, and she knew her stupid pale-as-milk skin was betraying the embarrassing fire his teasing innuendo lit within her. It didn't feel like he was making fun of her; it felt like he was flirting. Something deep within her rolled and somersaulted with . . . anticipation? Oh no, what was she thinking? Was she crazy? Had she forgotten all the pain he'd caused her? But her belly was full of the most delicious meal she'd had in a long time—that she hadn't prepared herself anyway. And the port had softened her normal stony reserve. And she was only human.

She smiled back. "Oh, boy, don't you worry. I will."

His eyes widened, and a slow grin creased his face as he gave her another thoughtful, appraising look. "I take back the stupid comment I made earlier."

"Oh yeah? Which one?"

Jackson laughed. "You're still Stevie Fox, all right, but you're not quite the same, not at all."

Before Stevie could decide if this comment should make her defensive or not, Jackson spoke quietly again—and almost made her heart stop. "I never did figure out why you started to hate me all those years ago, and I thought I was over it and didn't need to know. But now, seeing you again . . . can we talk? Really talk?"

The same server who'd burst into the kitchen to call for Jackson earlier—Melody—appeared again to say there was a problem with the debit machine. Jackson sighed and looked at Stevie. She didn't know what to say. It had been so long ago, what was the point?

The point is that how your relationship ended still bugs

you to this day, and you've never forgotten him, her brain lectured. Maybe talking it out will help.

Gah, she couldn't say any of that! She settled for, "Do you think you'll need a hand tomorrow night? I can probably swing it, around the same time, if you do."

Jackson's appraising look felt like it lasted forever when really it was no more than a split second. She shivered.

"Jackson!" Melody called again.

"Coming!" He got to his feet, then turned back to Stevie. "Anything that gets you here works for me."

"Okay then, tomorrow it is. Probably."

Jackson shook his head, but he was smiling. "Don't do that. Just come."

CHAPTER 6

I n some ways, Stevie couldn't believe it was only her second day at Cedar Mountain Lodge—or her first full one, anyway. Part of that was because of Jackson, for sure. It was bizarre. She hadn't laid eyes on the guy in over ten years. Then boom, in one evening—an evening that felt simultaneously like it was over in a heartbeat *and* like it had lasted a lifetime—it was as if that decade had rolled away. She was that same pathetic loser girl with a hardcore crush, bent on denying it and protecting herself—but at the same time, hopelessly drawn in, a glutton for punishment. And he was that same heart-crushing boy—arrogant, cruel, full of himself and all too aware of the power he wielded. Except . . . that perception of him kept nagging her. That view she'd held of him for so long—had been hurt by for so long. It didn't fit the man she'd re-met last night, and now that she was an adult too—and knew herself a bit, unfortunately—she had an awful worry.

What if Jackson had never been the terrible guy she'd built him up to be in her mind? What if all those awful things she'd put on him had been her own crippling insecurities and neuroses? Lord knows she had a zillion of each. But that would mean . . . what? That'd he'd been sincere back in the day? That he'd actually . . . No, that couldn't be it. It wasn't possible. Her self-esteem might have been in the toilet back then, but she wasn't nuts. His mistreatment of her couldn't be a figment of her imagination. And yet Jackson's face—his authentic-seeming surprise and bafflement when she'd warned him that she wasn't that teenage kid who'd take his bullshit—was imprinted in her mind. And he'd said he wanted to talk about that comment later—but not like he recalled the same incidents she did and wanted to apologize, more like he wanted to set the record straight or something as if *he* felt wronged.

Plus, there was his weird response to her compliment about his menu—his worry that *she* was being sarcastic or making a joke. Had she gotten him wrong all those years ago?

She wished she could run it past Maddie and Jo, get their take on it—but it wasn't fair to Alissa. And speaking of which, she'd better move. The lodge offered a ton of Christmas-themed activities on a repeating schedule every day, everything from cookie decorating and ornament making to skating parties and evening bonfires. Stevie was desperately hoping her sisters and Maddie would still be into taking part in various things throughout the week. It would be so festive and fun, and if they could convince Alissa to take part, it might help take her mind off her grief. But she was getting ahead of herself as usual. It was a vacation. They could figure out their itineraries on a day to day or even minute to minute basis. First things first—breakfast with everybody!

Unfortunately, "everybody" turned out to be inaccurate. Nan's back was bothering her, so she'd opted for room service. Alissa was feeling too low to show up at the café. Stevie, Hailey, Jo, and Maddie chatted happily enough but avoided the elephant in the room: the fact that Alissa was absent. Finally, after their breakfast arrived, Maddie broached the subject.

"I tried to get Alissa to come out this morning, but she wasn't up to it—wanted some alone time. She did agree to take part in some of the other things that the lodge is offering today, as planned."

Stevie sighed. Both Jo and Hailey looked at her, Jo looking concerned, and Hailey asking, "What?" with big eyes.

"Nothing really," Stevie said. "Just it's such a shame. If things were different, we'd have a blast up here together."

They all nodded in agreement, and for a few minutes, the only sound at their table was the gentle munching and crunching of crispy toast and bacon. Stevie pushed her Eggs Benny around her plate. The first bite had been delicious, but she was too heartsick to enjoy the rest.

When Alissa joined them in the afternoon, all Stevie could think as they toured the snowmen going up all over the place outside, had a family picture taken with Santa on a sleigh with real reindeer grazing beside it, and then found the cookie decorating station, was that it was really sad that things that should bring them so much joy felt more like a bereavement than a celebration.

"It's kind of surreal," Alissa said at one point as she piped delicate blue lines onto a snowflake-shaped sugar cookie. "I thought I'd be dizzy with joy today, getting ready for the biggest day of my life—well, second biggest day only to being united with you guys . . . Instead, it feels more like . . . I'm marking time to the anniversary of a death or something."

Her words so closely matched how Stevie felt that she was at a loss for something to say. She patted Alissa's shoulder helplessly.

Alissa clasped Stevie's hand for a moment. "Thank you for everything—especially the cheesy mac. At least that's one good thing, right? Since I have no need to fit into my wedding dress, I can eat with abandon." Alissa tried to laugh, but it was a strangled, painful sound.

"It's not enough. I wish I could do more. You should let me junk punch him."

Alissa giggled—genuinely—surprising Stevie and herself, from the look that immediately crossed her face after. She was immediately solemn again. "If I didn't think it would actually make me feel worse, not better, I'd tell you to go for it . . . but it won't help."

"I know. Nothing will."

Alissa nodded. "You're sort of right. Having you guys—knowing you'd do anything for me—actually does help, more than you know." She held up her pretty snowflake creation, glazed in white, trimmed in shimmery blue, and shining with just the lightest sprinkling of silver sparkles.

"It's perfect, just like you," Stevie said. "And if that numb-skull Jed can't see what everyone else can . . . well, maybe it's for the best you find out now, not later."

Alissa locked gazes with Stevie, and her tone was just as serious. "You're right. I just really believed in us . . . and I know how you feel—felt—about Jed and me. I guess I was really hoping to show you it could be done, that 'true love' is real."

"Not your job, buttercup," Stevie said lightly, again mysti-fied by Alissa's uncanny perception and feeling a little guilty. It wasn't Alissa's job to be a shining beacon of hope for her dumb, jaded ass. "And also, unnecessary. I already know true love is real. What our family has is as real as it gets. I don't need anything else."

Alissa nodded but looked wistful as she grabbed a new cookie—another snowflake—and continued decorating. And Stevie wanted to face-palm herself. She always said the wrong thing.

The day passed quickly, and although in some ways it turned out better than Stevie had anticipated it would when Alissa skipped breakfast, it was all too clear—especially as one by one, everyone said they had alternate dinner plans—

that the big family vacation Stevie had so been looking forward to was going to be drastically different than what she'd dreamed.

She wished Eddie was still around. An evening alone was never alone when she had him. And a walk never felt pointless. Finally, at her wit's end and tired of her endlessly looping thoughts, she found herself at Jackson's Pub.

It was hours earlier than when she'd told Jackson she might be able to show up, and how it might look—like she was desperate to see him again—was humiliating. Yet there she was, peering hungrily into the glowing yellow warmth of the place, regardless.

A solid figure all in black darted past the window—then backtracked and did a double-take. Stevie's stomach did a weird leaping thing. Jackson was standing there, looking at her.

He cocked his head to the side, and his eyes creased like he was silently asking her what the heck she was doing outside, staring in like a weirdo. She gave a one-shouldered shrug in reply. He grinned, shook his head, and motioned for her to come in.

Steamy heat blasted her as she opened the door, and laughter and voices spilled into the night air.

"Hi," she said, shrugging again. "I know it's earlier than I said I'd be able to chip in, but—"

Jackson cut her off. "Val—the woman you stood in for yesterday cooled off and is back to work, plus there's another cook you haven't met—Brandon—on tonight too, so thanks so much for your overly kind offer, but we're good."

Disappointment disproportionate to the situation surged through Stevie. Apparently, she—stupid, stupid her—had her heart set on working tonight. *Working*, her brain asked snidely, or seeing Jackson? A roaring heat that had nothing to do with the woodstove blazing away in the corner of the packed pub burned in her cheeks. And, to her utter humiliation, instead of just keeping quiet when nervous, her big mouth had to try to deflect. "Val, as in the madwoman who walked out on her shift—and you're fine with that? So, what, 'crazy shitshow' is your management style?"

Jackson looked momentarily taken aback. Then he laughed and scrubbed his chin—which had a delicious five o'clock shadow yet again, Stevie noted and hated that she did. "That's a pretty good description these days, unfortunately. But normally, no."

It hit Stevie then: Val and Jackson were a *couple*. That would explain the intensity of the whole dramatic walkout incident, along with how and why Jackson would take her back after insisting it was the last thing he'd do. She felt more foolish than ever—mostly because she hadn't clued in until this instant, despite knowing how attractive she still found him, that it really wasn't the chance to work and "get her mind off things" that made her come rushing back. Not even close.

"I'm glad your staffing issues are resolved. I'll see you around."

She turned to go, but movement in her peripheral caught her eye. She stopped mid-step just as Jackson said, "Wait."

She turned back and realized with another stomach-leap that he'd reached to catch her arm before she made it the door —then had stopped himself, probably realizing it wasn't that appropriate.

Jackson smiled self-consciously and motioned down at his body—like Stevie hadn't already checked it out. "Real person clothes today," he explained, sounding shy, "because I was hoping you would come by—and that I'd be able to convince you to take a walk with me or something. That's why I took Val back—and she is a good cook—and arranged for extra kitchen staff."

A tiny hopeful flame sprang to life in Stevie's middle, but she tried to tamp it down. It was one thing to admit to herself she had dumb fantasies about Jackson—as usual. It was another thing entirely to fool herself into acting on them. After how he'd treated her . . . was she a complete idiot?

Apparently, yes, because she found herself nodding. "That would be lovely."

"It would?"

She laughed at the blatant surprise in Jackson's voice and nodded.

"I mean, yeah, it would," he said in a deep, jokingly macho tone.

He went to grab a jacket, and Stevie wanted to pinch herself. This was . . . a surprise. But wait, the whole Val thing . . . she needed to be clear. Jackson returned in a fitted down jacket and black wool cap, and she pounced.

"So, wait, to be clear . . . You and Val . . . she's not your wife or significant other or something?"

"Val?" The level of horror in Jackson's voice was comical yet sounded sincere. "We've never been romantically involved in any way." He shuddered—a gesture that should've seemed theatrical, but again seemed utterly genuine, unconscious, even. "It's bad enough that I have to share my kitchen with her!"

CHAPTER 7

Snowflakes the size of quarters danced and twirled in a gentle breeze, and tinkling old-timey Christmas carols played through invisible speakers set up throughout the village, creating a festive but nostalgic soundtrack to Jackson and Stevie's walk. The snow flurry combined with the music and the scenery—each building they passed alight and twinkling—made Stevie feel like she was in a snow globe. The night was magical and impossibly pretty—and she felt every bit as fluttery as if someone had just picked her up and given her a good shake.

She and Jackson. Together—well, not together-*together* but walking and maybe going for a drink or for dinner . . . Talk about a blast from the past.

They moved in quiet unison at first. Then, once they were out of sight of the pub and away from the curious staff and prying customers' eyes, Jackson paused on the shoveled flagstones by an old-fashioned looking streetlight. The snowflakes swirling slowly beneath it were golden in its glow.

Stevie stopped walking too—the natural thing to do when the person you're strolling with quits moving.

Jackson openly stared at her for a long moment, and though Stevie knew it wasn't possible, he looked as awed by their being together as she was.

"*Stevie Fox*," he finally murmured. "I never thought this day would come—but for more than ten years, I always hoped it would."

A shiver that had nothing to do with the dropping temperatures of the mountains they'd found themselves in made Stevie tremble.

"Me too," she admitted.

"I . . ." He broke off and rubbed his chin. Definitely his tell, Stevie thought, realizing the gesture was already familiar to her. "It's just that . . . I think you owe me an apology."

Simultaneously, when Jackson had initially been at a loss for words, Stevie started to talk. "I always wanted—deserved an apology."

It took them a second, since they were both talking at once, to register what the other person had said, then Jackson said, "What?"

And Stevie, with equal confusion but a lot more bitterness, asked, "Are you kidding me? You feel *I* owe *you* an apology?"

"Well . . . yeah. I've worked through things, of course—I mean, we were kids, so a lot of what we went through comes down to that but still . . . I'd have done a better job of forgetting you if I'd ever had a clue what happened. Why you treated me so shabbily."

Stevie could only stare, her mouth agape, trying to grasp what she was hearing. Jackson thought she'd treated *him* "shabbily?" She shook her head. No, this was some bizarre gaslighting thing, and she wouldn't have it.

"You made my high school years hell—and trust me, I had enough problems back then without your added ridicule and constant mocking and—"

Stevie stopped talking abruptly, struck mute by the expression on Jackson's face.

"What are you talking about? I *never* made fun of you or mocked you." There was no way the confusion and shock in his low voice were faked. He was genuinely mystified. "I liked you so much. Maybe even . . . loved you."

"No way."

"Yes . . . way." Jackson's voice was as soft and heavy with emotion as brandy-soaked cake. "And I thought you felt the same way, that we were on the same page, but then your mom came to school that day, and everything changed. One minute we were . . . whatever we were . . . and the next, you hated my guts. It made my head spin."

"But you . . . " Stevie's brain stuttered as snippets of memories replayed. She remembered the day Jackson referred to all too well. The burning humiliation of it, the crushing pain of it, and—worst of all—how the minute it arrived, she'd realized she'd known it would happen all along. In fact, she'd been waiting for it.

It was the icing on a particularly disastrous batch of months. Stevie had gone to live with Maddie—and gotten her instant family of three sisters and a grandmother in the bargain—when she'd just turned thirteen. It was an instant family, but not instant stability—not for her anyway.

Unlike Hailey, Alissa, and Jo, Stevie wasn't an orphan, and adoption wasn't on the table for a variety of complex reasons. Marilyn was an addict and a drunk, who had deserted her daughter but also refused to terminate her parental "rights." Plus, CPS always worked toward uniting kids and their parents, keeping them together, whenever possible. But it wasn't just that, Stevie didn't lie to herself any more now than she had then. She'd spent most of her teen years feeling torn. She loved Maddie, called her Mom, and couldn't believe her luck and good fortune—that someone like Maddie would want her in her life, would choose her, would call her and her sisters "daughters of her heart"—so corny, but so awesome. And yet . . . she longed for Marilyn, her bio mom. Of course. As every kid did, whether their parent deserved it or not.

What did that say about her? Stevie had always wondered. Her sisters had their parents cruelly ripped away from them. If premature deaths or terrible accidents hadn't intruded in their lives, all evidence suggested they'd never have needed Maddie. They'd had families who loved them. She, on the other hand, was a person not even her own mother could love. Okay, intellectually, she knew that was not true—but emotionally, even now, it was very difficult, if not impossible, to not feel it.

Then, years later, when she had finally started to trust her place in Maddie's home and heart, to claim her family and let them claim her—her soft parts too, not just her prickly self-defensive side—Stevie's social worker, Natalie, had shown up with the "good news." Marilyn was back in town, clean and sober. And she wanted Stevie back. It was everything Stevie wanted for and from Marilyn—except that it also wasn't. Couldn't Marilyn let her live with Maddie and just get together lots with Stevie? Nope.

The first month was great. By the second, Stevie saw that her mom might be "clean," but her behaviors hadn't changed much—but older and with a part-time job, Stevie could get herself to school and eat, at least. Soon Marilyn realized that Stevie had cash and could "contribute" to the household. It was only fair, and also Marilyn's own job "sucked."

The first few lapses were rationalized and explained away by Marilyn as "not a big deal." She didn't even call them lapses. She just liked to "party," and seeing Stevie go out—as if her job at the Italian restaurant was "going out"—made her jealous. She was still young herself, after all. They were more like sisters than mother and daughter age-wise. Stevie didn't even bother to explain all the ways that was false—but she was also an ever-hopeful dupe and willingly chose to believe Marilyn when she said she "had things under control" and described the differences between "having a good time" and "having a problem."

Within six months, embarrassed and cringing—and praying Maddie had meant it when she said her home was Stevie's home, forever—Stevie managed to sneak over to Maddie's.

Over hot chocolate, Stevie admitted to Maddie that things were not going as well with Marilyn as Stevie had led her to believe. As an adult, Stevie realized Maddie had never been fooled—but as a kid, she'd thought she'd successfully sheltered Maddie from the truth.

Stevie had waited until it was too late, though. Marilyn had already had a public meltdown—and when Stevie got back to their apartment, the police were there. Stevie was taken back into care and deposited at Maddie's, shame and joy warring through her.

The "day" Jackson referred to took place a week later when an irate, totally out of it, Marilyn showed up at school.

"I'm just here to pick up my G.D. daughter, thank you very much," she snarled at everyone she laid eyes on. As an increasingly large crowd of students and teachers stared on in shock, she then commenced a screaming fight with voices in her own head, in between rants about Maddie that "expletive-expletive-expletive-expletive."

The police came—and took both Marilyn *and* Stevie away. An injustice that, even after all this time, still made Stevie feel like throwing up with helpless rage.

Thinking of the aftermath of that horrible time now, however, she tried to see it differently. When Jackson called right away after Marilyn's "show," Stevie had still been . . . utterly shell shocked and in pain. It was one thing for you to know you come from a train wreck of a family. It was another thing for the whole world to know. Was it possible she'd misinterpreted, misread everything he said? She remembered him saying, "You're so much like your mom, it's crazy,"—and then she *had* gone crazy.

Was it possible that he hadn't meant it how she'd heard it? And if that was the case, what did it mean about the other comments and actions—or lack of actions—she'd held against him all these years?

Jackson interrupted her creeping trudge down memory lane, his voice soft and soothing like he was trying to convince a feral cat not to bolt. "Fox, come on. Talk to me."

"Fox." That nickname—well, her last name—again. She'd always heard it with derision. Maybe it had simply been . . . what he called her.

There was so much she wanted to say, but her throat was clogged, making speech difficult. She was also increasingly aware of the intensifying chill in the biting wind that had kicked up. She inhaled as best she could through the grief and loss that was tightening her chest. Was Jackson right? Had it been her and her alone that had changed? Had she been the one who betrayed him, the one guilty, as he said, of treating him "shabbily?"

She sighed heavily. "I think my face is at risk of falling off, it's so cold."

Jackson's nodded once, looking deeply sad—but unsurprised.

"Can we . . . continue this discussion somewhere inside?"

Jackson's head jerked up, and his eyes flashed to hers. That had surprised him. Stevie gave a tentative smile. "Please?"

"Yes, yes, absolutely. I'd like that."

They made their way into Granite, the same bar she'd visited with Hailey the other night. Stevie glanced around in case her little sister's "plans" for the night involved handsome Nick and this same destination once more. If they did, Stevie didn't spot her.

They ordered drinks, and Stevie tried to explain how

unlovable she'd felt and how deeply ashamed of where she'd come from. Her words came haltingly at first, but soon flowed with ease. Jackson listened kindly and with grace— qualities she now remembered he'd always had, even though she'd talked herself into believing the opposite.

"When you witnessed that awful scene with my mom and the teachers, and the cops had to be called . . . I just thought I'd . . . well, I literally wanted to die, actually."

She had to look down at the table. The sympathy in Jackson's eyes was too painful.

"I couldn't bear that you saw the truth about me, and I was sure that you wouldn't like me anymore after seeing where—who—I'd come from. That first phone call, right after it happened . . . and you said I was 'just like her'? Well, I think I created a whole inner narrative—an incredibly negative one—about what that meant. I knew how I saw myself and figured that everyone else—especially someone like you —must feel the same way."

Jackson's face was flushed and distressed looking, even in the kind glow of the soft lighting. "I'm so sorry," he said roughly. "I'm such an idiot. I had no idea, but I should've. To me . . . well, it wasn't a big deal. I knew your mom was . . . problematic. I didn't think you took on any of her problems as your own."

"Don't be silly. How could you have known anything remotely of the sort unless you were a mind reader—and even if you had been . . . I hardly knew my own mind back then. It wouldn't have helped."

"No." He shook his head. "I knew there was something I was missing, something going on behind the scenes that I wasn't understanding, but my ego got hurt and I . . . reacted in kind."

Stevie nodded. They'd both spent months saying terrible things to each other—and about each other.

"It wasn't your fault. I had a ton of issues and deep problems. It's only been recent years that I even see what they are and how deep they run—"

"Still." Jackson shook his head again. "All that pain started over such dumbass comment. I should've known after the day you had, the last thing you'd have wanted was to be compared to your mother."

"Yeah," Stevie agreed. "It just never made sense to me, except to think that you saw something about my underlying personality that I hoped didn't exist."

Jackson had been about to take another sip of his beer, but he set the mug down hard and stared at her. "No, it was always about how uncanny it was to see her beside you. At a quick glance, you were like identical twins—only when you looked closer, you could see she was a bit older and, um, well, rougher." His voice lowered apologetically on the last word.

Stevie tilted her head in direct response to the topsy-turvy feeling his words induced. "What are you talking about? We look nothing alike."

Jackson let out a barking laugh—but it died as abruptly as it started. "Wait, you're serious?"

"My mom was, not that it helped her a day in her life, a beautiful woman."

Jackson nodded, studying her intensely as if waiting for a punchline. Then, when she just stared at him in confusion that was quickly morphing into irritation, he leaned in—still looking like he was the butt of a joke. "And so are you. You've always been super . . . beautiful. You know that, right?"

Stevie shook her head, unable to form a response.

"You just said your mom is beautiful."

"Uh-huh?"

"Well," Jackson's tone grew serious as if all this time he'd really thought she was having him on and only now realized she wasn't. "You do know you look just like her."

It genuinely was news to Stevie.

"How pretty you are . . . it's why I always called you by your very fitting last name, of course." Jackson grinned, but he looked suddenly unsure as if maybe he'd screwed up again in some big, unknown way.

"Huh," Stevie said. "I always thought you were making fun of my looks or being sarcastic about my hair or something."

Jackson shook his head.

After a moment of silence, Stevie spoke again. "Well, this is awkward."

Her hand was resting on the table between them. Jackson took it suddenly, squeezed it, then released it. "It doesn't have to be. We were kids, and we were idiots—or I was at least. It's good we parted ways back then before we could do an even worse number on each other."

"It is?"

"Definitely." The cocky confidence Stevie remembered in Jackson of old made an appearance with his dimpled grin. "I was thrown when you didn't respond to my attention by being as into me as I was into you—but I think I can remedy that now."

"Oh, you do, hey?"

Jackson winked. "Absolutely."

A server popped around to check on their drinks, and Stevie was suddenly famished. "Do you want to eat?" she asked.

"Always."

She grinned and asked the server for menus.

A long while later, their appie plates long-cleared, and their meal of potato-wrapped halibut in white wine sauce and savory tomato basil pie long-demolished, the server returned to their table.

"It's last call. Can I get you anything else?"

Jackson and Stevie's eyes flew to the metal clock—an

abstract piece of art featuring giant cogs and sprockets. "No, thank you," Jackson said.

When the server left, they raised their eyebrows in shared amusement and mingled awe and disbelief. They had been talking for hours. About serious things. About silly things. About a lifetime of experiences that as teens, they'd promised to share together—then vowed not to. Now, with nostalgia, they found themselves sharing without any anger or recriminations.

They'd discussed what they'd done the past ten years, where they'd trained, places they'd worked, spots they'd traveled to for fun—and to cook—and how she, and now he, always found themselves back in Granite Ridge.

"It sounds like you've built a good life and had a lot of adventures," Jackson observed at one point.

"Yes," Stevie agreed, marveling a bit, as she always did, at the truth of that. To her surprise, she added, "I'm a little lonely these days, though, with Ed gone so recently."

"Oh? I'm so sorry. I didn't realize . . ." Jackson sat back in his chair and straightened a little. "How long has he been gone? Do you think you'll get back together? Do you want to?"

His response baffled Stevie for a second—but then she understood. Jackson thought Ed was an ex-boyfriend or even an ex-husband.

If Ed were still alive, the misunderstanding would've been funny. As it was, she was horrified to feel her eyes well.

"He was my dog, but also my best friend. Is that dumb?" She brushed at her eyes roughly and shook her head. "I'm . . . sorry. I don't even know why I brought him up."

"Because we're getting to know each other," Jackson said softly and reached for her hand again. "And I'm surprised to find myself saying this, but now I wish Ed *was* some pain-in-the-butt competition. I'm very sad your dog friend died."

Somehow it was the exact right thing for him to say. "He would've thought it was hilarious that you were jealous."

Jackson grinned. "I was, though, wasn't I?"

Spilling her heart to Jackson felt as natural as it ever had—before she'd wrecked everything that is, but she wouldn't focus on that now.

Jackson smiled at her again, then shook his head. "I still can't believe . . . you're here. With me. It's like no time has passed between us in all the best ways. I don't want the night to end."

So why does it have to? Stevie wanted to say, but she wasn't sure she was ready, however much she wanted to be, for what the comment might be taken as an invitation for.

"Unfortunately, I have a super early morning tomorrow. I need to go to town for supplies to see the pub through until the new year, and then I'm having dinner with my dad."

His voice hardened slightly, and Stevie realized something with a pang. It sounded like Jackson still had issues with his own parent, and while they'd talked about her family—or families—she hadn't asked about his.

She was about to stammer out some sort of an apology, but the server was back. Jackson handed over his credit card, waving off Stevie's insistence that she chip in.

"You can buy next time." He winked, and something warm and happy zipped around Stevie's stomach. There was going to be a next time. She was going to see Jackson Basset again. She'd confessed how neurotic and messed up she was, and he'd . . . forgiven her just like that.

They bundled back into their coats and scarves and hit the cold again. At the corner where Jackson would turn left to go make sure the night's close had gone smoothly, and she'd continue on straight toward the overnight parking, Jackson turned to her. "So yeah, busy all day tomorrow, unfortunately—but I'm off the next day if it works to get together again."

"I want to jump up and down and say yes, absolutely."

"But?"

Stevie sighed. "But it depends on how everything's going with Alissa and everyone. I need to be—I want to be, I mean —at their beck and call, able to help any way I can."

"I totally get it. Same old fox, same old henhouse, hey?"

Another old joke—but this time Stevie couldn't understand how she'd ever heard it as anything except silly and cute. It definitely wasn't a criticism.

"You're lucky to have them."

Another thing he'd said back then—that she'd misconstrued, taken as an insult like she wasn't worthy. Before she could beat herself up too badly, he distracted her from her bad habit of self-loathing.

He was staring at her mouth—then his eyes, so full of heat she could barely feel the night's chill, met hers again. "May I?"

So, so many echoes of the past—of *their* past—it was dizzying. All those years ago, the first sweet time they'd kissed, Jackson had asked permission back then too. So different than the other experiences she'd had with boys then and with men since.

She lifted her face to him, smiling, a thrill of anticipation like candy coming to temperature bubbling through her. "Please do."

Even knowing it was coming, the kiss took her by surprise —well, not the kiss. Her body's response to it.

His lips brushed hers as if bidding farewell—but then, as she leaned into the action, he pulled her closer and pressed in, mouth soft as velvet on hers at first. Such a simple, innocent touch—that sent fireworks of desire rocketing through her.

Her mouth opened to him without tangible thought, and his tongue danced against hers. Oh, how Stevie had missed this. Had missed him!

They finally pulled apart, somewhat ruefully, almost as if

slightly embarrassed by how hotly their lust for each other still burned after all these years.

"Stevie Fox," Jackson breathed. "I'll be damned."

She knew what he meant—and shivered as his hand slid down her jacketed arm, caught her hand, tugged it lightly, then released it. "Okay, well . . . until we see each other again then."

"Yeah," she agreed stupidly, then grinned when he did. As she watched him saunter away, her heart continued to race— and her sense of surprise ratcheted up higher. She really hadn't built up her reaction to him in her mind over time. Their connection really was . . . something else. So many big questions abounded. Should she let herself enjoy and explore it? Or should she be grateful she and Jackson had cleared up their misunderstandings and now leave him firmly and fondly in her past, no longer a source of distant pain—and not a potential source for any future pain either?

CHAPTER 8

Despite being up late the night before, Stevie woke bright and early, happy about a day of Christmassy activities with her sisters. Then she checked her phone and discovered to her chagrin that Nan's back had flared up again, and Maddie was driving her to the doctor in Granite Ridge. Alissa had asked for the day to herself, and both Jo and Hailey were also mysteriously busy.

She was tempted to pull the blankets over her head and go back to sleep. Instead, to her monumental annoyance, she found herself thinking about Jackson again. *Missing him.*

What's wrong with you? she chided herself. You're not a heartsick teenager anymore, pining away for Jackson Basset. You just saw him last night, for Pete's sake!

The inner lecture did nothing to curb her thoughts, however, and she even grinned a little. So what if she wasn't a teenager? She hoped she never got too old for crushes—as long as that's what they stayed. Nice, safe *crushes*—feelings that were by very definition brief because their focus was on someone inappropriate or unattainable. Jackson, in a nutshell. But anyway, her longing was a waste of time because he was away today, shopping, then visiting his dad. Would he be up here for the rest of her stay, or would he be taking off again for Christmas? What did he and his fancy pants dad do for the holidays? Something spectacular?

The first Christmas she knew him, he and his dad had spent three weeks in the Bahamas. He returned as toasty brown and yummy looking as a gingerbread man. He, however, had seemed almost jealous of her cozy—noisy!—family Christmas. Stevie had understood completely. It wasn't a lack of stuff or absence of vacations that made life with Marilyn difficult, so she easily saw how the reverse could be true. Fancy possessions or trips also wouldn't make up for life with a difficult parent.

As if cued by Stevie's thoughts, her phone pinged, and Jackson's face and number flashed, announcing a text. She opened it, her heart thudding and her mind filling in possible nasty messages like, *I don't know what I was thinking with that kiss,* and *I never want to see you again.* That wasn't what the note said, however. Not even close. She really was her own worst enemy.

"I miss you," he typed.

Another message pinged. "Sorry if that's too much, too soon, but it's true."

Stevie found herself grinning like a loon. Before she could reply to either text, however, her phone dinged a third time. "I won't be back till late, and I'll be out of cell service shortly. Just wanted to see if you're still a night owl and if you want to hang out tonight."

The idea of seeing Jackson again—let alone the fact that he'd been the one to reach out and say he missed her—sent a rush of giddiness bubbling through her like champagne. She let her fingers fly without censor. "If you're silly, I am too. Was totally thinking about you too! Would love to hang out tonight. Any time that works for you. Am busy with my sisters but will watch for your text. Drive safe!"

Stevie hit send. Instantly, her delight fizzed away, replaced by neurotic insecurity. Why had she been such a blabber-mouth? Who sends a novel via text? What was wrong with her? What was she thinking, being so effusive? He was going to see how much he meant to her and how little she'd changed. How on earth could that be a good thing?

Stevie didn't get a chance to keep berating herself, however, because her phone buzzed four more times in quick succession—two texts from Maddie, two from Hailey. She read each message with disbelief verging on horror. No way. Absolutely not! This wasn't happening. It made less than no sense. It had to be a joke. *It had to be*. Her fingers flew once more.

"Are you kidding me? NOT funny."

Maddie's reply was swift and immediate—and hit like a cast iron frying pan: The wedding was back on. For real. And Maddie wanted them to meet in her room for a family meeting later.

Stevie couldn't stop stewing. What was Alissa thinking? *What?*

By the time she and her family wrapped up, Stevie still hadn't heard back from Jackson, but that made sense. He'd said he wouldn't get back until late, and it was barely eight. She headed back to her RV to have a quick, very non-luxurious shower. Earlier, she'd planned to pamper herself in Jo's suite soon, but speaking of that, Jo had been remarkably closed door with her suite despite her earlier offer that Stevie could use it. She was as warm as ever, and if there was one relation-ship Stevie was confident about, it was her and Jo's . . . Yet still, if she hadn't known better, she'd worry Jo was mad at her or something. She'd even expected to have a sleepover in Jo's room, so they could stay up yacking half the night . . . but Jo was always busy. Maybe she was "up to something" as she liked to jokingly accuse Stevie of being. Normally the thought would've made Stevie laugh out loud and genuinely hope that she was. On the heels of Alissa's decision, however—a terrible one, Stevie feared—she wasn't in the mood.

Feet planted on the heavy-duty rattan welcome mat that she always placed at the base of the pullout steps outside her home-sweet-traveling-home, rain, snow, or shine, Stevie was fumbling in her bag for her keys to unlock the RV's door when her phone rang. She hit talk without looking and didn't bother to disguise her glee. At least Jackson was a bright distraction.

"Perfect timing! I just left everybody. I'm all yours."

A throaty, nervous chuckle, followed by a low-timbered rasp that would've filled any 60s or 70s rocker with envy, filled Stevie's ear. "Stevie?"

Stevie's stomach plummeted. She'd recognize this voice anywhere, of course—and it was decidedly not Jackson. She could kick herself for not checking who was calling before she answered.

"Stevie?" the voice repeated.

"Marilyn . . . Hi."

"What? You don't call me 'mom' anymore? You're too old for that or what? Or let me guess, you call Her mom now."

As always, intentionally or with the dumb but unerring knack for cutting to the quick some drunks and addicts have, just two seconds into the conversation, Marilyn had managed to jab one of Stevie's most sensitive parts. Even now, after not living with her for fifteen years, except for that short, awful stint in high school, Stevie struggled with what to call her mother the rare times they had contact.

Stevie corrected herself, hearing the weariness in her own voice. "Hey, Mom. What's up?"

"Does something have to be 'up' for me to want to talk with my baby girl at Christmas?"

Marilyn was obviously drunk and feeling belligerent and

confrontational. It was like she was spoiling for a fight when they hadn't even seen each other since Stevie's last birthday.

"Of course not. Merry Christmas, Mama." Mama. Oh, how easily Stevie fell back into this insipid, weak version of herself, desperate to keep the peace at all costs and maybe, just maybe, earn a pittance of affection or an affirming word. This was precisely why Stevie battled with what to call her. Marilyn had been right when she accused Stevie of calling Maddie "Mom"—and why shouldn't she? Maddie was her mom in every good sense of the word, and yet, unfairly, Stevie often felt torn there too, and alternated between calling Maddie by name or by Mom, as well. The difference between the two women was that Maddie didn't mind. But even that made sense and made Stevie's loyalties squirm. Maddie's place in Stevie's heart was locked in. Permanent. Marilyn had to feel—or worry, at least—that her role was more precarious. It wouldn't matter that it was all her own doing. In fact, Stevie could understand if that fact only made it harder.

She sighed heavily, turned the key in the knob, and let herself in. Throwing her purse onto the tiny dining table, she settled into her "reading chair," a pint-sized 70s velvet recliner at its avocado green finest that she'd salvaged from a curb, eons ago. Draping her legs over one of the chair's arms, she took a deep breath. "How are you, Mom? Are you doing okay?"

Seemingly mollified by the usage of two moms and a mama in close succession, Marilyn's tone softened and grew syrupy. "I'm hanging in there, baby girl, hanging in. You know how it is."

And yes, Stevie thought she did know how it was—but that didn't earn her a reprieve. Marilyn proceeded to share a litany of hard-luck stories and bad boyfriend tales—the latter, this go-round, about someone named Hank. Stevie hadn't heard of Hank before, but she knew she'd already met him several times. Marilyn had a distinct type of man she went for, but that she never recognized as such until it was too late.

The minutes turned into a quarter of an hour, and Stevie grew aware of salty trails on her cheeks, making her skin itch. Moving her face away from the mouthpiece for a moment, she sniffed hard, then moved closer again. Marilyn was still talking. For a moment, sadness stole Stevie's ability to speak. She cleared her throat.

"Look, Mom. It was good to hear from you, but—" What excuse could she use that Marilyn wouldn't take blistering offense to? "I have to work." She glanced at the vintage sun shaped wall clock she'd hung over her small gas stove. It wasn't totally unbelievable. "I've got a gig at a posh-as-heck ski resort pub. You'd love it. Split shifts though—" She shut up. She was talking too much. It would give her lie away.

Marilyn must've had another drink while they were talking, or else she already happened to have enough alcohol in her system to see her through to her next predictable phase of inebriation. The doting mom.

"I'm so proud of you, honey. My daughter, the traveler. The chef. The adventurer."

"Yeah, yeah. Listen, I've got to—"

"Run. I know it." Marilyn suddenly sounded less blurry, more focused. "Before you do, honey, I just wondered if I could beg a huge favor. Things are super tight for me right now, what with going into Christmas, you know how it is."

Again, Stevie did. She really did.

"And rent's due, and—"

"How much do you need, Mom?"

"Just a little to tide me over. Hank's got a great job, just they're on shut down right now."

Stevie didn't say anything, and after a moment, Marilyn mentioned an amount that made Stevie's eyes widen. Shoot, she'd thought she was beyond being surprised. She had a savings account that she wouldn't touch for anything except maybe a business in the future. In fact, she almost blocked its existence from her own mind, having her bank automatically move a percentage of every deposit into it, fearing that if it was too present in her thinking, Marilyn would somehow intuit its existence. But her regular day-to-day account was pretty healthy. She lived pretty lean—what did she need except food, after all—and Marilyn hadn't called in a while. She could afford it.

"I'll send it when we hang out," she said softly.

"To this phone number?"

"By text, yeah."

Marilyn hung up without saying goodbye.

"Mission accomplished, hey?" Stevie whispered and stared out the big window that formed a dark backdrop to her little dining space. Early by workers' or vacationers' standards, the camping area was quiet, quiet, quiet.

She checked her phone. No other texts or e-mails had come in while she was talking to Marilyn, and she got to her feet in a rush, suddenly desperate to cook. She needed to get out of her head, to be taken far away in scent, texture, and origin.

About to wash her hands, Stevie remembered her promise to Marilyn. She retrieved her phone again, logged into her bank account, and sent the transfer.

"Merry Christmas! Wishing you all the best in the New Year!" she typed in the little message box. It was a fine enough wish—for a friend or acquaintance. It felt sad and impersonal for your mother.

Even before Jed revealed himself to be a big douche canoe by breaking up with Alissa, Alissa hadn't wanted a full-fledged bachelorette party. She had agreed, however, that a foodie "girls' night" would be fun. Stevie had made lists of her sisters' favorite appetizers and delectable bites—much the way she'd planned movie night treats back in the days that they all lived together. When the wedding was canceled, Stevie had done a full shop anyway, thinking, hoping, her treats could soothe a broken heart. She should've known better. And now, with the stupid wedding back on with no days to spare, there still wouldn't be a good time. Oh, well. At least, it meant she had oodles of ingredients on hand to make whatever she craved. Or craved food-wise, anyway. If only other desires in life were as easily assembled.

Stevie rooted through her fridge and pulled out a chunk of fresh ginger root, a grapefruit-sized green cabbage, and a package of ground pork—lovely and fatty. Then she rummaged in her spice drawer and withdrew a head of garlic from the natural clay pot she stored it in and a jar of pink Himalayan sea salt. Next, she rounded up sesame oil, soy sauce, and cornstarch. Finally, she took a small pair of scissors and snipped a big clump of garlic chives from a recent—only? —splurge a few months back: a hydroponic herb garden set up.

Chopping, mincing, grating . . . Her mind stilled with the familiar work, and her nerves calmed as the good, strong, healing aromas of garlic, ginger, and sesame were released into the air while she built the filling.

Some people might think it was cheating to use pre-made wrappers, but Stevie didn't and grabbed a package of her favorite brand from the fridge. The work surface atop her chest freezer, freshly wiped down, of course, and now dusted with flour, soon filled with row upon row of plump, perfect crescents.

While she worked, she daydreamed the way she always did when she cooked. Tonight, she was far away from where she was now, maybe in a foreign city's kitchen, where someone would taste her humble offerings and never believe she wasn't a local, that she didn't belong.

It was silly, sad even, for someone her age to still comfort herself so often with make-believe, and yet, she couldn't be too hard on herself about it. It was a better coping mechanism than a lot of other things adults fell prey to, right?

She retrieved a heavy-bottomed skillet and set it to medium-high heat with a tablespoon of oil. In her imagination, she accepted compliments from her new boss as he surveyed her creations. Then she popped back to reality again for a minute. The way she loved food but had no specialty, nothing that set her apart from anyone else who was good in the kitchen . . . The way cooking for her was often a way to stay a kid and play pretend. Pretend you're really a fairy princess banished to a foreign land because of the sins of your parents. Pretend you have magical powers, that each dish you make is really a powerful spell. Pretend, pretend, pretend. . . . It was why she'd never amount to much "professionally"—at least in other people's eyes. Cooks who became "executive chefs" or, to those under them, just "Chef," the ones who had their own kitchens and went on to have famous restaurants, had deep cultural heritages to pull from, a history of cuisine and family lore that "informed" their cooking, a tradition that, pun intended, fed their culinary creation. Stevie had none of that.

It used to bother her and make her feel like less at the schools she'd attended and kitchens she'd worked in. Cooking merely because you liked food was . . . lame. She'd been a hungry kid—and now she was a hungry adult, craving comfort and connection and . . . fun. But over the years, she started seeing her perceived flaw or lack as a strength.

She could make almost anything she set her mind to. She loved reading other people's menus and concocting stories from the food they assembled and put together almost as much as she loved reading fiction. Because for her, it was the same thing. And she felt lucky about that. Much like the aspiring ballerina who realizes she'd rather teach classes and dance in a small theatre for the fun of it, Stevie loved that she didn't care about fame or prestige anymore. Plus, as long as humans needed to eat, she'd never be out of work.

While her pan came to temperature, Stevie deftly filled a cookie sheet with gyoza, holding twelve back for herself. She'd put the tray in the freezer, then transfer the frozen gyoza to an airtight container. They'd keep, frozen, for months and be good-as-fresh whenever she pulled them out to make in the future.

Soon the RV was filled with the mouthwatering scent of frying food. Stevie threw together a simple but perfect dipping sauce: soy sauce, rice wine vinegar, and a generous splash of chili oil. She arranged the gyoza on a square platter decorated with red poppies, then poured the sauce into its built-in vinegar dish. The crispy bottomed dumplings were gorgeous even if she did say so herself, and her mouth watered, imagining their silken texture on her tongue. She grabbed chopsticks and sat down to eat.

An imaginary man across from her—who looked a lot like Jackson, come to think of it—lifted a mug of tea in salute, and a little girl with his wavy dark hair exclaimed, "Yummy!"

Stevie smiled back, savoring her first bite and its explosion of soft, complex flavors.

As she ate, however, her daydreams receded, and the events of the day flooded through her. Alissa's grief—and now her, to Stevie's huge worry, decision to give Jed another chance. Marilyn's ongoing mistakes, yes, but equally undeniable suffering, so often in the search for love, however misguided. Jackson's promise to call or text tonight, so they could hang out . . . She found herself hoping he didn't. Even Maddie, so brave, so strong, chose to embrace single life rather than risk all that pain again. If someone like Maddie couldn't bear to face a relationship, what hope did Stevie have?

She'd just finished the dishes and was giving the freezer's

work surface a final wipe down when Jackson texted, as
promised. She read his words, frowning.

CHAPTER 9

Bundled up against the cold, Stevie walked back to the main village to meet Jackson. From their brief exchange of texts, she could tell that he was a bit surprised she wanted to meet outside and go for a walk. Initially, he'd said he'd come to her, and earlier in the day, inviting him into her RV for a cozy night of visiting would've been like a dream come true. Now, however, she didn't want him in her home. It was . . . too much. Nothing would come of them connecting again after all these years, and she wasn't going to make seeing him into something it wasn't. Then he'd suggested she come to his place.

"No funny business, I promise," he texted—then sent another message immediately on its heels with a winking emoji. "Unless you want it, that is."

"No, let's meet in the covered courtyard by the ice sculptures like I said or not at all."

"Okay. SYS."

Stevie stared at Jackson's abbreviated text. *See you soon* —the very idea would've thrilled her even a few hours ago, but now it made her anything but. Why was she even bothering to meet him when now she knew for sure she wasn't going to pursue anything?

At first, she didn't see him. Her full attention was caught by the ice sculptures, which were somehow even more awing in the night than they had been during the day. Maybe because no other people were milling about, distracting from their magnificence. Or perhaps because as soon as it got dark, large bright colored spotlights were turned on, making each work of frozen art shine vivid blues, greens, purples, pinks, and golds. Whatever the reason, it was like being in a magical world. Her favorite was a glass-like menagerie of animals decorating a huge Christmas tree. A close second was a cowgirl, complete with a Stetson hat and lasso, riding a rearing unicorn and smiling widely.

"Hello," Jackson's low voice came from behind her—and like a ninny, she shrieked.

"Sorry," he said, laughing. "I didn't mean to startle you." His happy expression faded when she didn't smile back. She couldn't. Seeing him again, she wanted to melt into his arms. How pathetic was that? They didn't even know each other. Not really. It was something Marilyn would do—build up some big imagined relationship in her mind, then be crushed when surprise, surprise (to her only!) it ended up being nothing, or worse, something that ended disastrously.

"Is there something wrong?"

"No," she said tersely and started to walk, no longer seeing the statues in such a romantic light. They were just big blocks of ice, nothing lasting. They'd be gone without a trace as soon as the season changed.

Jackson hesitated, then caught up and fell into step with her. "All right, if you say so, but you seem . . . different. Your text earlier sounded like you were as happy and eager about getting together tonight as I was. Now you're acting like you're doing me a favor. You didn't have to come out."

Stevie shrugged, bitterly disappointed in herself. Why was

she such a coward? She was being really unfair, but she didn't seem to be able to stop. And here she'd thought she'd grown so much since high school. All it took for her to regress to her angry, cowardly ways was a call from her mom and disappointed worry for her sister.

"Did your sisters say something about me? Do they not like me or something?"

"Of course not. I haven't told my sisters about you. Why would I?"

"Um . . . well, just I know you have this perfect, close-knit family. I thought you told your 'soul sisters' everything."

Stevie stopped walking abruptly and turned to stare at Jackson. "Are you making fun of me? Of my sisters?" She felt crazily close to tears.

"What?! *No*."

"Good because it wasn't perfect. We all came from nothing. Had *nothing*. It's a miracle that we were united, and it's not a laughing matter."

"Clearly," Jackson muttered. When Stevie didn't reply, he sighed heavily. "Look, I don't know what I did to get off on the wrong foot tonight, but I've obviously done something wrong. Whatever it was . . . I'm sorry."

"It's fine. Don't worry about it."

Jackson pushed his hands through his wavy hair. "It seems like you're cutting me off. Ending our relationship or something."

Stevie laughed. "What relationship? Dude, I helped cover a shift at your restaurant, and we hung out once. How's that a *relationship*?"

She tried not to think about the sweetness of their recent kiss—or how even just recalling its steamy heat set her insides to simmering again.

"I . . . " Jackson's voice trailed off as he studied her. Stevie forced herself to slip away inside, knowing that doing so made her face as impenetrable as stone. Finally, he sighed. "Okay, well . . . see you around."

"I doubt it." Stevie forced a lightness she didn't feel into her voice. "I had some spare time these past few days, but Alissa's wedding's back on, so things are going to be busy from here on out."

"Wow." Jackson shook his head, his voice, low and sad. "You are just . . . *wow*." He jammed his hands in his pockets and hunching against the cold—or against her—he strode away.

Stevie's heart hammered so hard it felt like it might bruise her sternum. This wasn't what she wanted either. "So, what? You're just going to walk away?" It came out sounding accusatory—not how she felt, which was gutted with disappointment in herself.

Jackson froze, then pivoted to face her. A blue spotlight shining on a six-foot-tall bouquet of ice roses lit him up. The cold light created the illusion he was made of ice, too—or maybe it was just the hard chill in his expression. "Yeah, that's exactly what I'm going to do." And he did.

Throat aching, Stevie used every ounce of her willpower to not race after him. She'd only try to apologize or explain herself. Yes, she'd been, was *being*, inexcusably rude and ignorant—mean, even. In fact, she was acting exactly the way he'd said she had as a teenager—but so be it. As shameful as it was, it was for best. If someone as sweet and good and kind as Alissa couldn't find love that lasted—at least not without the equal chance that it would decimate her in the process—what chance did a mess like Stevie have? She'd wrangled a safe and mostly satisfying life for herself, and she wouldn't risk it. She couldn't. Not even for Jackson Bassett. She squeezed her eyes shut for a moment, trying to block the memory of Jackson's hurt, confused face and warm, kind eyes. His affection seemed so genuine . . . like all the worst traps always did.

CHAPTER 10

S tevie awoke, grouchy and out of sorts, and decided to have a home day, which was another definite perk of RV living: you could hide out, wherever and whenever. She needed time to convince herself that distancing herself and Jackson was the right decision—and to try to come to terms with Alissa's decision.

"Bad zzzz's last night. I'll see you guys later," she group-texted everyone, including Alissa.

Wrapped in a quilt on her bed, eating crispy sourdough toast with butter and crabapple jelly that glowed like amber jewels, she perused the Internet for rescue dogs in need of homes. See, she told herself. That's a lovely fantasy that could actually become a reality: a new dog baby is definitely something you can pull off. She'd always miss Ed, of course, but it was time. And even if he'd still been alive, he wouldn't have minded a buddy.

When she was done breakfast, she brewed a pot of Kicking Horse coffee. She was addicted in the best of ways to the small Canadian company's Three Sisters blend—a robust medium roast that made her think of campfires, late-night chats, and fresh air adventures. Then, sipping from her favorite mug, she lifted the dining table's bench seat and retrieved the cylinder-shaped container that held her Christmas tree. Another thing it was time for.

The wee little tree wasn't even two feet tall and had come pre-wired with tiny warm white lights that danced and dimmed in various patterns set with a small remote, getting brighter or more twinkly, then fading away and starting again.

Stevie placed it on a wide shelf above the kitchen counter she'd installed for this very thing—seasonal decorations—and anchored it in place with the tie-down system she'd come up with. No doubt she'd stash the tree again before moving on, but just in case, it was good to have it secured. She gathered her small box of ornaments and the swath of purple satin she used in lieu of a tree skirt from the bench seat cupboard. After wrapping the shimmering fabric around the base of the tree in a loose flourish that hid the base and tie-downs, she took out each of her precious ornaments—little marvels received over the years from Maddie and her sisters—and hung them with care. Even after all this time, she couldn't pick a favorite. She loved them all, from the tiny cast iron frying pan with the spray of miniature holly leaves, complete with berries, to the small snow globe depicting a forest scene —a mama deer and little fawn in a copse of pines—to the surfing Santa Maddie sent by mail the one Christmas Stevie hadn't been able to make it home, the year she'd spent working at a resort on the barrier reef in Australia.

Last, she draped a string of lights across the back window of the RV in a soft scallop shape, using the tiny hooks she'd installed last year, and hung a small wreath in the center. She plugged in the lights, then clicked her little tree's remote. Her RV sparkled to Christmas life. Even in the gray light of day, shining nowhere near as brightly as they would at night, it was pretty and cheery. She freshened her coffee and tried not to think about how nice it would be to share her cozy home with someone. And not just a four-legged someone. And not just a generic someone. She was definitely obsessing about Jackson again. It was the only damper to her peaceful and very needed quiet morning of puttering and homemaking. No matter how much she pretended differently, he was never far from her thoughts.

"But you took care of that temptation," she muttered. "You showed him once and for all that you really are as messed up as he thought you were."

Breaking ties before she got hurt was the goal, so why did the fact that now she didn't have to worry about Jackson breaking her heart seem like the very heartbreak she'd hoped to avoid?

She shook the thought away and ran her finger gently over the shining face of another ornament—a stunning silver Christmas locket, almost as big as the hollow of Stevie's palm, featuring an etched snowflake inlaid with Swarovski Crystals that sparkled as they caught the light. The back was hand-stamped with the year Maddie had gifted it—and identical ones—to her and her sisters. Stevie didn't have to open the beautiful doodad to see the faces in the picture it held. They were ingrained in her memory as surely and permanently as the snowflake that decorated the beautiful keepsake. She did open it though and smiled down at their younger selves, a great upwelling of love and gratitude moving through her.

And thinking of her sisters and Maddie, just like that— slam! She was forced to think about Alissa's on-again wedding, which she'd successfully managed to avoid most of the day. She had five good places to sit and an abundance of food. What she wanted more than anything was to invite them over to dine chez Stevie tonight. Instead, she was going to have to suffer through some horrible "apology dinner" that Jed had arranged for them all, as a way to try making amends. She supposed she should get ready for it. Barf.

❆

Stevie met up with Jo by the doorway to the hotel's big dining room and couldn't help but voice one more grumble. "This is complete lunacy!"

Jo didn't disagree exactly, but as ever, she was more diplomatic. "It's her choice, though. We need to support her."

"What do you call this?" Stevie motioned down at the clothes she was wearing, a spaghetti-strapped navy silk jumpsuit and flats, paired with a dove gray Pashmina wrap—the latter a purchase to go with the dress she'd gotten for the wedding. "I'm going, aren't I? This is . . . support."

"Yes, and you look lovely."

"I don't want to look lovely. I want to look armed and dangerous."

Jo laughed, and Stevie sighed. "I. Can. Not. Believe the wedding is on again. I just . . . can't."

"She loves him."

"It's not *her* love I'm questioning, and let's be real. Since when is love ever enough?"

Jo bit her lip, looking as pensive as Stevie felt, and although Stevie buttoned her mouth as they walked in to find their table, she must've radiated anger because people kept staring—and then looked too obviously like they were trying not to.

Stevie surveyed the large room glumly, and their reservation immediately jumped out at her: a huge round table, beautifully set with ivory linens and a centerpiece of mixed flowers.

Her throat throbbed, and she looked up, focusing on the ornate chandeliers overhead and willing away tears. She rarely wore makeup, and it would be just like her to end up looking like a feral raccoon when she was trying to present well and not disappoint her family.

A gentle tug on her hair jerked her attention away from

the ceiling. She turned to see Hailey, who beamed at her and then gave her an exaggerated once over. "You look gorgeous. You should wear your hair down more often."

"She even blow-dried it," Jo chimed in.

"Ooh la la, that is fancy."

"Stop it," Stevie growled.

"And I love your outfit. It's fabulous. You look like such a grown-up."

Despite how self-conscious Stevie felt in such girly clothes, she had to grin a bit at that. "Well, we are grown-ups, so that makes sense."

"Yeah, it's totally weird," Jo said.

Laughing with her sisters went a long way to soothing Stevie's angst—until Jed walked in with an absolutely glowing Alissa on his arm. Alissa caught sight of Stevie across the room. It was like time stopped for a split second as Alissa communicated a complicated barrage of commands and pleas to Stevie, via widened eyes and a concerned expression.

Stevie gave her a nod of reassurance and flashed a peace sign. Alissa smiled gratefully but still didn't look completely reassured.

"It's like she's worried I'm going to stab him," she whispered to Jo.

"Aren't you?" Jo whispered back.

"Not while there are so many witnesses hanging around."

The awkwardness of the situation surrounding the upcoming meal made the comments seem funnier than they were. Jo, Hailey, and Stevie all stifled giggles as they made their way to the table where Jed, Alissa, and Maddie were already seating themselves.

Jed immediately stood to greet them as they approached. Hailey and Jo were their gracious selves. Thankfully, a server appeared at the table, so Stevie could turn away before Jed made eye contact or reached to shake her hand, without it being a blatant snub. Not that she'd personally mind Jed feeling slighted, but she would hate for Alissa to feel it.

Dinner did not get less awkward from there—for Stevie, anyway. She couldn't believe how everyone ate up Jed's syrupy apology. Adding too much sugar was how food manufacturers attempted to disguise low-quality ingredients, and she couldn't understand how his lines didn't leave a bad taste in the family's mouths, the way they did hers. And Alissa? Her newly restored happiness and transparent hope- fulness made Stevie feel like she might literally bleed with pain and worry for her. It collided too much with the memo- ries she had of Marilyn's many, many "this time it's different" stories. Yes, she was projecting, but still . . . she was wound up so tightly with anxious thoughts she could barely enjoy the company of her sisters.

Finally, dessert arrived. Her sisters were still savoring theirs, when Stevie, after a few mouthfuls, pressed a hand to her stomach.

"I can't swallow another bite," she said truthfully—and didn't just mean about the food. "And I'm not feeling the best." Again, not a lie. "I'm sorry, but I need to duck out."

She said her goodbyes to a murmur of collective concerns, adding, "No hugs, in case I'm contagious." That was mostly a moot point as she wasn't a big hugger anyway, and her sisters weren't expecting them. Still, Jed and Alissa had both risen in their seats. Stevie wanted to stave off any chance of having to endure the hypocrisy of letting Jed hug her. She couldn't believe she'd shared once recipes with him so he could "treat" Alissa. She was a sucker too. Not as big a one as Alissa, apparently, but still. She was almost out of the restaurant, home free, when Maddie caught up with her.

"Can I talk to you for just a second, sweetie?"

"Of course. What's up?"

Maddie looked at her for a long moment, and Stevie prepared herself to hear how if Alissa could give Jed a second chance, Stevie should certainly be able to do the same . . . And it wasn't like Stevie couldn't see that point; she just didn't like it. But no such encouragement was forthcoming.

Instead, Maddie was speechless and pressed her hands to her mouth, looking stressed. Concern zipped through Stevie. Maddie was normally unflappable.

"What is it?"

"I'm just," she shook her head, "a bit frazzled. We need a venue for the rehearsal dinner. Our original choice is booked solid now, and a zillion other things are vying for my attention. After the rehearsal dinner, I have to zip down to Granite Ridge and—"

"Cross the dinner off your list. I'll handle it. Don't worry," Stevie heard herself promising before her brain could veto it. "And I'll keep you company on your drive afterward, too—help keep you awake."

"That's sweet, but how? It's Christmas at a ski lodge. Reservations have been set for months, and—"

"Don't worry," Stevie repeated. "Consider it done."

"There's so little time. . . . Can you really pull it off?"

"Yes," Stevie said confidently.

"Okay, if you're sure—and don't worry about the cost. Jed has confirmed that he'll be paying for it."

"Wow, how big of him. I'd expect nothing less—because it really is the least he can do."

Maddie patted her hand and sighed. "I know you're concerned on Alissa's behalf, but sometimes people genuinely deserve second chances—and they don't let you down."

"Mmhm," Stevie said, but she was only half-listening now, her mind churning. She wasn't lying to Maddie. She could definitely pull off the rehearsal dinner, but it would mean begging the favor from Jackson he'd promised the night she'd helped out in the pub. And that, of course, that meant . . . seeing him and apologizing to him.

CHAPTER 11

"Hey . . . It's me. Can we talk?" Stevie texted.

She waited for half an hour without receiving a reply from Jackson. Under normal circumstances, she'd assume he was busy and would think it perfectly fine to not hear back for hours or even a day or two. Modern society's expectation of instant responses was usually something that drove her crazy. But tonight, time was of the essence. Plus, even before hitting send, it was something she'd been afraid of and knew she deserved: him ignoring her if she made contact.

"I owe you an apology. Please let me make it in person."

Crucial minutes ticked by. It was almost eight-thirty. The later it got, the tougher it would be to ask if she had any hope of using his pub. And if he said no, or it wouldn't work for some reason, the more difficult—if not impossible—it would be to arrange it somewhere else.

She tried one more time. If Jackson still wouldn't respond, she'd swallow her pride and show up in person at the pub. "And I have a huge favor to ask—but no pressure on that front. I was a jerk and want to explain and say how sorry I am."

She was about to leave the lodge's warm lobby and go track him down when her phone finally pinged.

"I'm at the bonfire."

The bonfire. Stevie knew about that. The lodge's event schedule mentioned a bonfire "party" every night in December, with vendors offering various seasonal goodies.

"On my way," she replied, choosing to ignore that his wording was probably intended to convey he was busy, rather than being an invitation to join him. She stuffed her phone into the inside pocket of her down-filled coat—no more lightweight jackets for her, too cold! Then she did up her zipper and made good on her word, heading out into the chilly night to find Jackson.

It wasn't difficult to find the bonfire. If she'd somehow missed the pretty sparks shooting like mini fireworks into the velvet sky or been blind to the soft swirl of smoke drifting upwards, the noise of the roaring fire and din of the lively crowd would've drawn her to the spot.

As she got closer to the outdoor party, other scents and aromas tickled her nose, adding to the cozy woodsmoke and creating a festive feel: mulled apple cider being served from the back of an old-fashioned looking wagon, rich chocolatey hot cocoa steaming in a huge cauldron on an outdoor stove, sugary roasting marshmallows, spicy sausages turning on a food vendor's spit. . . .

Stevie wished she was only there for the fun of it, could just find Jackson in the crowd, slip her hand into his, and watch the fire, while sipping a steamy cider . . . but she'd wrecked that possibility with her hardheaded retreat to the Stevie of old: self-protective, snarky, her own worst enemy.

She inhaled sharply when she spotted him, and her desire to touch him spiked even higher. This time, however, she wasn't motivated by simple lust or the less noble hope of getting to skip an uncomfortable conversation. No . . . she wanted to offer comfort. He seemed in need of it. He was standing alone at the outer edge of the crowd gathered by the fire, his face half in shadows, half in light. He looked as handsome as ever, but also deeply sad about something.

As if sensing her analysis, he turned suddenly and scanned the gentle flow of comers and goers. She lifted her hand in greeting, not expecting him to notice her straight away. He did, though, and gave a terse nod, then wove his way toward her.

"Oh, *Jackson*," she exclaimed, sounding embarrassingly melodramatic and formal.

Her greeting made him crack a small smile, however, so maybe it was worth sounding like a weirdo—and he mimicked her tone. "Oh, *Stevie*."

He still looked sad though, and his arms were crossed over his chest, his stance evaluating, not friendly, so despite his tiny bit of teasing, Stevie didn't feel out of the woods yet. "Can we talk?"

He shrugged. "Sure. Talk away."

"Umm, maybe somewhere quieter? More . . . private?"

Jackson studied her face, and something unreadable—by her anyway—moved like a shadow behind his eyes. "Why? What's the point?"

"Please? Just indulge me one more time. I know I don't deserve it."

Stevie endured another long, uncomfortable moment of study. Finally, Jackson sighed. "Fine."

He uncrossed his arms, jammed his hands into his pockets, and started walking at a rapid clip. Stevie hurried to keep up, and it became clear after a few minutes that he was taking her back to the pub. It was a slow night, with only a few tables full. No doubt, it would fill up as the bonfire wound down. He led her to a small table by the big Christmas tree, which acted like a privacy screen.

"Would you like something to drink?"

She would but thought maybe she should see how the conversation went first. She was really worried for him.

"Not yet. I want to say a few things, then we'll see. I'm hoping after you hear me out, we'll be friends again." At that, Jackson let out a small derisive noise, but Stevie pressed on, trying to ignore how it felt like her heart was shriveling in her chest. She tried to insert hope she wasn't sure she actually felt into her voice. "And then, yes, I'd love to share a beverage with you."

She sank onto her chair and cracked her knuckles. Where should she even begin? The plain, simple truth was probably best—but then again, "truth" was rarely either of those things.

When she still didn't speak, Jackson beat her to it. "I was super excited when we crossed paths again. You were definitely built up in my mind as the 'the one who got away,' so seeing you here? Like a jackass, I . . ." His voice petered out, and he didn't finish saying whatever it was he was going to confess.

Stevie cringed. She had the power to make him feel bad? All the way back then, when they were practically kids? And now, still? It defied everything she'd ever believed. And she never would've hurt him intentionally. "I have no good excuse. I was—I *am*—super excited to reconnect with you too. I was thrilled by the idea of spending more time together, but then my mother called and, as ever, it threw me. She still has the power to reduce me to this unhappy, angry, anxious kid, who's absolutely sure nothing will work out and that no one could really care about her." She sighed, hating to reveal how lame and weak she was, but also relieved to share the truth instead of trying to act like someone she wasn't. "She's still . . . such a mess—a mess who's always sure the next guy will be her salvation. Thinking about her—and all the Alissa-Jed complications—I got . . . cold feet. Thought why bother starting something that won't work out anyway? Thought it best to burn the bridge before either of us started very far across."

Jackson didn't say a word. Just watched her with narrowed eyes, his jaw tight. And Stevie realized that in addition to the myriad little things she'd screwed up in the short time they'd been reacquainted, there was something big, something important, she'd been deeply wrong about too. After hanging out that first night, she'd thought he hadn't changed at all, but he had. Back before everything went wrong between them—or, more accurately, before *she'd* went wrong between them—she'd been able to read Jackson like a book. He was always so open, confident, and just completely . . . transparent. In a good way. Now she couldn't read him at all. He'd become super skilled at hiding his emotions, thoughts, and feelings. Had she done that to him? Or was it just becoming an adult that had changed him?

"Um," she said to fill the uncomfortable silence between them, "not that you'll be able to tell or anything, but I actually have grown a lot since we used to know each other, just occasionally all my freaky neuroses come out to play again." When he didn't smile at her attempt at levity, she sighed again. "I really am sorry. It's no surprise to me that I'm still messed up when it comes to some kinds of stuff, but I really didn't mean to make you feel bad or to hurt your feelings or to imply that you aren't . . . totally great."

Given how their conversation had gone so far, she wasn't expecting the big easy smile and immediate understanding and forgiveness Jackson had extended to her time and time again when they were young. Still, the flat, unmoved expression in his eyes and tightness in his jaw unnerved her.

"We're not kids anymore," he said. "And you're not the only one who gets scared or whose challenging relationship with their parent colors their view of the world."

Stevie recalled the sad expression Jackson wore when he was unaware anyone was looking. She'd always thought his issues with his dad were small potatoes, but maybe they'd grown over the years. Mr. Bassett had always been hard on his only child and held brutally high expectations. A son who wanted to cook for a living didn't exactly fulfill them. But she didn't get a chance to ask what he meant, specifically. He spoke again, and his words burned painfully, hot as oil splatter from an overheated skillet.

"I think I overly romanticized what we had. Overly romanticized you."

Stevie swallowed hard and nodded. She wanted to look away, to stare at the floor, or over his shoulder, or anywhere that wasn't this hard.

"I forgot how your off again, on again moods damaged me, controlled me."

His words cut deep, plunging a sharp blade of self-awareness deep into her center. Had she turned into her mother, into Marilyn, despite all her best efforts and work not to? She pressed her hand to her mouth to hold back a stricken yelp, wanting to weep.

On his side of the table, mere feet from her—feet that might as well have been miles—Jackson seemed oblivious to the effect his observation had on her. He continued to drum his fingers, focused on some point beyond her, like he was in the middle of deep, agonizing thought, trying to make a decision or come to terms with something. Then suddenly, abruptly, his eyes flashed, and he pinned her with his gaze once more. "Did it mean anything to you? Anything at all?"

"It?" she asked, genuinely baffled.

"The kiss. Our kiss. When I kissed you—and you, you kissed me back." It was like an accusation, and she could see the pain of rejection in his eyes, as clearly as looking into a mirror.

For once, her body—her heart, her flesh—overrode her brain. Without a pause for thought or self-doubt or over-analyzing, she grabbed Jackson's restless hand. "Of course, it did. Totally. In fact, if anything, it meant . . . too much. Just now, I blamed my mother, but really, I was—I am—just scared of myself." She laughed nervously. "I mean . . . I have a special talent for alienating people I care about."

"You mean your mom?"

"No." She shook her head. "You—all those years ago. And again . . . now."

This time, the long, contemplative look he gave her didn't feel as unfriendly.

"I probably overreacted."

"No, the things you said were fair."

He nodded. "Except, I left out the important part."

Stevie thought she'd taken about as much painfully honest criticism as she could handle, deserved or not. "Oh yeah?"

To her surprise, a twinkle of the old Jackson reappeared. "Yeah. I forgot to say that even at your batshit craziest, Mad Madam Mim wackiest, Maleficent grouchiest . . . when I was at my most confused or frustrated, I always loved your honesty about your struggles, and I've had more fun, more passion, in the times spent with you than I ever have with anyone else."

He flipped her hand suddenly so that it was sitting in his palm up. Then he traced the inside of her exposed wrist gently with one finger like he was writing something there. She shivered, and he looked up, smiling. "Also . . . I know you don't believe me, Fox, but you're so pretty, so, damn, damn pretty."

Something hard and resolute inside Stevie crumbled a bit. Not the whole wall, mind you, but definitely some of the supporting timbers. She didn't know what to say on the heels of that, exactly, so she settled for, "Mad Madam Mim and Maleficent, hey? *Nice.*" She rolled her eyes but felt happy. "Speaking of passion, that's something I loved about you. Our shared obsession with Disney movies."

"See? Deep down, I knew there were things you loved about me."

Not that deep down either, Stevie's brain piped.

Jackson grinned like he'd heard her thought, then half stood and beckoned a server close. "Can you bring us a bottle of the Catena Malbec?"

"A whole bottle? We must be friends again, then," Stevie said, her tone light and flirty—a good disguise for the deep excitement and joy rioting through her.

"No," Jackson said solemnly, settling back into his seat— but pulling the chair closer to hers as he did. "Or, I mean, yes —but never just that. We're doing this thing, Stevie. No pressure. As slow as you want . . . but we're seeing where we go. As adults."

"But I thought—I think—I'm too much of a mess for you."

It was Jackson's turn to looked shocked, and then his handsome face filled with chagrin. "*That's* what you took away from this conversation?" He shook his head. "That's the furthest thing from what I was trying to say. I was just trying to figure out where I stood . . . and setting boundaries. I'm always out of my depths when I'm with you, and I like it— love it—but I'm old now. I can't handle the roller coaster. I need you to tell me what's going on in your head, explain when you're worried or freaking out, so we can deal with it together."

Stevie smirked. "Setting boundaries? Sheesh, you *are* old." But she couldn't hide her happiness—and she didn't want to. "Thank you for accepting my apology, Jackson. I look forward to . . . being friendly."

His eyes glinted. "Oh, good because we're going to be friendly, all right. Very, very friendly, I promise you."

A frisson of heat thrilled through her. Jackson had always been good at keeping his word.

Halfway through the bottle of wine and a plate of to-die-for steak bites with a side of sautéed crimini mushrooms,

Jackson asked, "What's the favor, by the way—or was that just a ruse to get my attention?"

"Shoot!" Disbelief tore through Stevie, a hard, bracing chaser after the sweet, headiness of the wine. Of Jackson. "Right. I can't believe I forgot. I was totally distracted."

Jackson had moved even closer while they ate and chatted, and his thigh was a warm solid weight against hers. He turned in his seat. "Fair's fair," he whispered. "You're always distracting me."

She wished she could forget about the marriage-on-again debacle and rehearsal dinner dilemma and keep enjoying the moment, but the mood had shifted. Reality had successfully intruded. Rats. She said as much, and he laughed. "Don't worry. We're, this, it's all still pretty unreal."

"Alissa's wedding is back on. Jed showed up, so sorry, a totally changed man, blah, blah, blah."

Jackson shook his head, then drawled in an exaggerated Southern accent, "I do declare, Stevie Fox . . . It's almost like you're jaded or something."

Stevie laughed despite her newly refueled stress. "So anyway, long story short, my mom and my sisters are in a panic to resurrect all the canceled plans. Most things are coming together, but the venue for the rehearsal dinner is booked solid—as are the lodge's other restaurants."

"That's rough, but I'm not sure what I can do."

"Can we have it here? It's a fantastic venue, and the cook's okay—" She waggled her eyebrows.

"The cook's *okay*?" Jackson clutched his heart as if wounded. "Ouch! If this is how you go about trying to get a favor, I can see why you're struggling."

"Okay, okay, in real life, the cook is fabulous, and the food is amazing."

"The 'cook' is a prodigiously talented genius, whom you should call *Chef*, I'll have you know," Jackson said in his best snootiest highbrow tone, but then his voice grew serious. "I'd love to say yes, but we're going to be swamped tomorrow. There's a big family reunion here at the lodge, and they called ahead. We're reserving half the place for them."

Stevie scrunched her face. "I suspected that'd be the case, that you'd be busy. Could we possibly, if it's not too much to ask, use your staff table? It's the right size, and the way it's slightly tucked away from the main action is perfect."

Jackson's eyes lit up. "Of course—great idea. I'm glad I thought of it."

"Uh-huh." Stevie felt herself twinkling back at him, just like the best of old times. "Your staff won't mind?"

"Nah, we're all so busy with different things this time of year, we rarely have a family meal. Normally we do something together to celebrate the end of the holiday rush sometime in January."

"Normally?"

He looked sad again. "My lease will be up by then—but never mind. That's a boring topic for another day." He motioned with his hand like he was literally flicking something away. "Now, if we're going to pull this off right, we have some major planning to do."

CHAPTER 12

T wo more sleeps until it's Christmas, fa-la-la-la-la, la-la-la-la, Stevie's brain sang on giddy repeat as she entered the lodge and made her way toward the restaurant where she was meeting her family minus Hailey, who had a prior engagement, to finalize the plans for the next few days. Despite her misgivings about the on-again wedding, walking past the magnificent tree, lovely greenery, and festive displays in the lodge's huge foyer, she felt like a kid looking forward to Christmas. She wasn't self-deluded enough to think the bubbly euphoria rising through her was simply caused by the approaching big day, however. It was the prospect of spending most of the day with Jackson—under the guise of "rehearsal dinner prep," of course. She would be spared being teased and harassed because her lovely sisters would never suspect a thing!

Alissa and Jo had beaten her to the restaurant, and Stevie made her way to the table and sat down, undoing her wool coat, but not taking it fully off.

"Are you wearing makeup *again*?" Alissa squinted in disbelief.

"She is," Jo confirmed.

Alissa leaned in, studying Stevie like she was some unfamiliar yet intriguing food dish. "And your hair is curled again too."

"I'm wearing a ponytail," Stevie scoffed.

"Yeah, but you have lift in the front, and the actual pony's all gently waved and has a little flick at the end."

"You're getting married in one day," Stevie said. "Don't you have better things to obsess about?"

Alissa grinned prettily. "Absolutely not. You're hiding something. What is it?"

Jo lifted an uncharacteristically saucy eyebrow. "Or *who*, more like it?"

So much for avoiding being teased. But it's not like her sisters actually knew anything. They were just stabbing about in the dark—and no doubt hoping to keep Stevie from harping about Jed. "I'm just trying to put a bit of effort in like you guys are always insisting I should."

"More and more suspicious all the time!" Alissa chimed to Jo, acting like Stevie wasn't even there.

Stevie scanned the small dining room, looking for a server, any server. If they could order, they'd all be distracted.

"Hey, you guys," Maddie said, appearing beside the table —later than the rest of them, which was unlike her. What's up with that? Stevie wondered, then was distracted by Maddie's completely obvious once-over. "Look at you! What's the big occasion?"

"Would you guys all please stop acting like I never groom myself," Stevie grumbled and craned her neck, looking for the server again.

"Uh, you rarely do 'groom' yourself. You consider a shower primping," Alissa teased.

"Ha ha," said Stevie.

Jo couldn't resist chiming in again too. "You consider a long sleeve T formal wear."

"Hilarious! It's too bad you're such a great lawyer because you're a natural comedian."

Jo and Alissa laughed out loud.

"Seriously," Jo added, not coming to her aid one bit, "you're wearing a cashmere sweater and a push-up bra. What gives?"

Stevie's face flamed, and she yanked her jacket closed to hide the soft V-neck revealing her—admittedly slight—cleavage. "Assholes!"

"Language!" said Maddie. She undoubtedly meant the gentle rebuke, as she had ever since Stevie was a mouthy kid, but she also sounded amused.

One of the things Stevie loved about having a family was how corny and silly you could be with them. Here they were all in their twenties, Jo—crazy!—thirty already, and they still acted like kids a lot of the time. It was the best part of having siblings—and maybe the worst, too—how you were perpetually children with each other. She wondered where Hailey was, feeling sad she was missing out.

"Fess up!" Jo commanded.

Stevie widened her eyes innocently. "Whatever do you mean?"

"I already told them by accident," Maddie explained.

Wait a minute! A lot of things were immediately clearer. "Told them what?"

"That the rehearsal dinner's back on and that the man helping make it happen is none other than your old beau Jackson."

"Are you kidding me?" Stevie groaned, but there was part of her that loved their silly teasing affection. "There is nothing between Jackson and me. Less than nothing."

"Uh-huh," said Alissa, eyes shining. Then she chanted in a singsong voice, exactly the same way she had when she was little. "Stevie and Jackson sitting in a tree, K-I-S-S-I-N-G!"

"Really?" Stevie said as Jo and Maddie laughed. "You're

going to be a married woman, and you're singing about me kissing in a tree?"

"Absolutely," Alissa said. "And speaking of me becoming a married woman, I'm going to be doing a lot more than kissing."

The group guffawed. "Now, that's a song for me to sing!" Stevie said. "Alissa and Jed, married in a tree, F—"

"Don't you dare!" Alissa giggled.

"I wouldn't," Stevie assured her—then winked. "Or would I?"

"You would not," Maddie said sternly, but laughed. "Or you better not. I mean it."

The server, perhaps lured by their singing, lest more of it continue, finally showed up. Brunch proceeded in a blur of chatter and last-minute confirmations of renewed plans. Before Stevie knew it, they were all standing up and rushing off to do whatever was next in their list of wedding-related tasks.

As they all filed out of the restaurant together, Alissa pulled her aside. "Thank you for handling the rehearsal dinner for me. I know you're worried and you don't think I'm doing the right thing, but—I am."

Stevie looked at her little sister for a long time. She was actually surprised that not once, as far as she knew, had Alissa asked any of her sisters what they thought about her taking Jed at his word and starting the ball rolling on their wedding again. She'd talked to them a lot, but she was standing on her own two feet and listening to her gut. In short, Alissa was being precisely the strong, decisive, independent person Stevie knew she was, even though in the past, Alissa had shared she sometimes doubted she had those qualities.

"It's no secret that I was furious with Jed. Still am. And honestly, if you feel he needs a good punch, I'm in."

"You can't—"

Stevie held up her hand. "Don't worry. I love you, so I won't do anything to embarrass you. Also, you love him, you're standing by him, and I trust you, so . . . if he's okay with you, he's okay with me."

"You mean it?"

Stevie nodded and wished sincerely that her thoughts on the matter were as simple as her words suggested. "I'm happy for you, and I want you guys to have every single happiness forever." That, at least, was one hundred percent unequivocally true.

"Thanks, big sister." Alissa's misty eyes made Stevie choke up.

"It's just you're so special, A," she said, using a nickname from their childhood. "I hope Jed really gets that. Knows it. Will live it."

Alissa nodded solemnly. "I believe he does. That he will—that we will."

They were silent a moment, then Stevie lifted her arms at her sides and let them drop with a big exhale. "Well, then, that's that." She smiled and willed herself to look joyful.

"There's one more thing," Alissa said, chewing her lip.

"What?"

"Our beautiful cake." She looked on the verge of tears again—and not for happy, sentimental reasons this time.

That rotten little worm! Stevie ranted inwardly. He'd told Alissa about the cake. Probably even showed her the pictures. Gutless rat—

"He showed me the groom too," Alissa confirmed.

"He deserved that—and more," Stevie blurted without thinking. She was about to backpedal, but Alissa surprised her by grinning.

"Yeah, he totally did."

They both snickered, and then Stevie patted Alissa's shoulder, a tad awkwardly. "Anyway, don't worry about it.

I'm making you another cake. It will be simpler but equally lovely."

"Are you sure? You don't mind?"

"Are you kidding? I'm honored."

Alissa, not the awkward, hug-averse weirdo Stevie was, pulled her into a tight clinch. "You're the best. Thank you."

It was the furthest thing from the truth. Every single one of her sisters was better than her. Still, Stevie appreciated the sentiment, and her heart filled with the compliment. Maybe she didn't have everything she dreamed of familywise, but she had more than enough with Maddie and her sisters. She was lucky.

They were about to part ways when Alissa said, "So is Jackson still a good K-I-S-S-E-R or what? And don't even try to tell me you have no idea."

Stevie rolled her eyes—and Alissa's giggle followed her out the door.

When Stevie walked into Jackson's Pub using the kitchen entrance just before noon, the whole place was already filled with the rich aromas of roasting meat. If the delicious scent was anything to go by, the rehearsal feast was coming together seamlessly, which made sense because she and Jackson had put together the menu the night before. Lucky for them, Alissa and Jed both loved barbeque—anything and everything country, actually—so coming up with food they'd enjoy, but that wasn't difficult to prepare, was easy. Plus, the necessary ingredients were common fare, so Jackson had everything they needed in stock—including ribs and a huge pork roast because of a special he'd planned for the New Year "farewell" dinner. It felt meant to be.

She said hello to the two dishwashers and greeted the salad and desserts person, happily surprised by how warm they were toward her. It made her feel like Jackson didn't have strange women drop by the restaurant very often, as if she was special.

Jackson wasn't anywhere to be found in the kitchen, but she located him in his office—standing with his back to the open door, looking over papers of some kind, with a sort of rigid stress in his posture.

She crept in and reached up, sliding her hands over his eyes. "Guess who?"

He jumped, literally, and dropped the sheaf of papers he was holding, which made her feel a bit bad—but not so bad that she didn't laugh out loud.

He left the papers where they lay on the desk and turned, smiling.

She checked her watch. "I'll have to duck out by 4:30 or 5:00 for the actual rehearsal, but I'm all yours until then—and again, after, of course."

Jackson quirked an eyebrow suggestively. "Don't kid yourself, Fox. You're all mine all the time."

He was only joking, of course, because sure they were "seeing where things went," as he'd said, but it wasn't really serious. It was just flirting, wasn't it? She wished for more, but she knew better. Still, his words made her whole body feel light and airy.

She thought again of their kiss and had a moment of regret. Not about the kiss itself—but about the fact that there hadn't been another one yet. As if reading her thoughts, Jackson reached out and touched her face, running his fingers down her cheek. "It's not the right time or place, but I have to say I can't wait until we have all this family stuff of yours behind us, so I can distract you to my heart's content."

Stevie laughed—a bit breathlessly because of the bubbling heat that lightest of touches sparked within her. "Promises, promises," she teased.

He locked eyes with her. "Absolutely."

The heat ratcheted up—too high. She had to look away, then step away, or they'd never get anything done.

All through the afternoon of prep, cooking, and saucing—and baking the cake, which she'd decorate the next day—Stevie was filled with anticipation. Soon she and Jackson would have time, well and truly to themselves. Soon, soon, soon.

As they worked in the kitchen's close quarters in perfect sync, exactly the way they had that first night she'd helped out, how easy Jackson was to be with continued to awe Stevie. She just felt . . . at home in her skin whenever she was with him—skin that zinged whenever he was close! Every so often, they exchanged a look that felt like a physical touch. Even Stevie, as neurotic and insecure as she knew she too often was, could tell Jackson was looking forward to being alone as much as she was.

The rehearsal itself went smoothly, and the dinner afterward was better than Stevie could've been imagined. The pub, though full to bursting with the family reunion guests as Jackson had said it would be, wasn't overly loud. Everyone was more interested, it seemed, in catching up and sharing stories than in revelry. Hence, the rehearsal party was intimate and private, with a lot of physical—and mental—space for their own conversation and memory spinning. And the food? The food was amazing. They ate family style, which was super fitting, of course—for the group, but also for the type of meal it was. Alissa couldn't stop praising it, and Jed ate his body weight in ribs, coleslaw, pulled pork, and slow-cooked beans. His hearty appetite didn't even bother Stevie. It made her happy, in fact.

After eating until they could eat no more, they all tried their hand—or feet, rather—at learning to line dance, which was hilarious fun.

No one could've been more shocked than Stevie was to realize she was having a great time—though she knew part of her enjoyment was fueled by the knowledge that every delicious bite and every dance step taken was getting her closer to enjoying downtime with Jackson.

Except that . . . it didn't happen. As the evening drew to an end and Stevie was close to turning pirouettes at the idea of seeing everybody head out, much as she loved them, Maddie approached. Her face was awash with gratitude—and something else.

"Thank you so much, sweetie. Dinner was wonderful, and it made Alissa so happy."

Stevie glanced over at Alissa, who had already hugged her goodbye and was now standing near the door, tucked into Jed's side, gazing up at him with an expression of laughing adoration. She bit her lip. "Yeah, I'm glad everything turned out."

"Are we still on for our whirlwind trip back to Granite Ridge to get my dress for the wedding?" Maddie continued. "And don't let me forget to grab my garter too. I really want Alissa to wear it. It's the one I wore at my wedding—the same one that Nan wore at hers. It will be her something borrowed *and* her something blue. I didn't bring it because . . . " She trailed off because she and Stevie both knew why she hadn't thought it would be needed.

Jackson's smile flashed in Stevie's mind, and her stomach lurched painfully—exactly the way it would've if she hadn't eaten all day and was finally about to have a meal, only to have it disappear on her. She'd totally forgotten her earlier offer to accompany Maddie on her late-night trip. Still, she ignored the dash of regret that sprinkled through her and didn't hesitate. "Of course. Let me just . . . thank Jackson and his staff again and grab my jacket."

She ran back through to the kitchen and found Jackson reorganizing the walk-in cooler to make room for leftovers from the night. He took one look at her face and said, "Aw, rats, I'm being ditched, aren't I?"

"Yeah, but you know, not like ditch-ditched."

"Not ditch-ditched?" His eyes crinkled. "Well, that's a relief."

She smiled back and explained the errand Maddie needed her to ride shotgun for.

"I get it, but it totally sucks. I was looking forward to—you know. Hanging out."

"Me too."

He took one of her hands in his cold ones. "Enjoy your time with your Mom—Maddie?"

"Either, both, I use them interchangeably."

Jackson nodded. "We'll have time soon. This is important."

She nodded. It was, and she appreciated him for understanding and not feeling stood up. "Thank you."

"Until tomorrow then. . . ."

"Yeah."

For half a second, Stevie thought he was going to kiss her again, finally—but then Melody, the server Stevie met her first night at Jackson's, appeared. "One of the family reunion guys wants to thank you in person."

Jackson sighed again and stepped back. "I'll be right there."

As Melody darted way, Jackson grinned and whispered, "They can't separate us forever. In the end, we will prevail!"

Stevie laughed—just as another server, one Stevie hadn't met personally, appeared. "The till tape's out, and I can't find the box of replacements in the storage room."

Stevie widened her eyes and shook her head in exaggerated but silent disbelief, which made Jackson crack up. On the way out of the office, he caught her arm, then slid his fingers down and linked hands with hers. He gave one gentle squeeze in farewell.

"Travel safe," he whispered. "And come back to me a lot sooner this time than the last time you left me."

Stevie nodded and couldn't believe how torn she felt. She usually welcomed any and every chance to hang out with Maddie, and she knew they'd have a great time. And yet . . . her entire being seemed to resist as she strode away from Jackson and went to find her mom.

CHAPTER 13

The alarm on Stevie's phone started to sing. She stirred in her comfy bed, reveling in the soft warmth of her sheets and quilt—and in the yummy dream about Jackson that she didn't want to end. She rolled over, then pulled the blankets over her head, hoping to block out the alarm and snuggle back into sleep. Less than a minute later, however, she bolted upright. It didn't matter that she'd been up until almost 3:00 in the morning and it wasn't quite 6:00. What was she doing sleeping in? It was Christmas Eve! And Alissa's wedding day. She had stuff to do.

She clambered from her cozy nest, threw on sweatpants and a long-sleeve T-shirt, and pulled her hair into a messy bun. Yes, she'd been putting in an effort since she'd started spending time with Jackson, but with everything she had to do—and considering the reality that if they were going to be together a lot, sooner or later, he'd remember the slob she naturally was—there didn't seem to be much point in making a fuss just to go decorate a cake. Besides, she was going to have to endure a whole afternoon and evening in a formal dress, complete with nylons of all things. Gag! She might as well enjoy being comfortable while she could.

Typically, Stevie was a fan of a healthy breakfast to give her energy to last through a busy day, but Maddie's amazing cookies called to her, and it was Christmas Eve. What kind of holiday season would it be if she didn't suffer a couple sugar overdoses and energy crashes? She snapped open the container of cookies that were quickly disappearing and munched one down in quick bites, delighting in the familiar and beloved sensation of the crispy, crunchy outer layer giving way to a soft center and explosion of rich chocolate on her tongue. She ate a second cookie more slowly and still couldn't decide, as ever, which way she preferred: the wolfing it down method or the slow savoring. Either way, Maddie's double-chocolate chocolate chip cookies were out of this world. It drove her crazy how, no matter how many times she tried to duplicate Maddie's recipe, her version was never quite as good. Over the years, she'd hounded Maddie for the secret ingredient she must add, but that wasn't written down.

Every query got the same response: Maddie's playful smile and a wink. "All my Mom love—and there's no substitute."

Stevie was still smiling at fond memories of Maddie, many of them centered on cooking and doing other chores together, as she locked up the RV and headed out.

It was still dark, and it felt like the temperature had dropped another twenty degrees. Stevie found herself running, not walking, to Jackson's pub, where she would decorate the cake, having already gotten the go-ahead from him by text the night before. By text! Why on earth weren't they just spending the night together!? Like maybe not "spending the night" spending the night—not yet; it was a bit soon, maybe—but just like, being in the same location, for the night.

"You are a freak!" Stevie said aloud to the slowly light-ening sky. She hadn't noticed a group of snowboarders nearby, walking with their boards and helmets. They gave her a weird look, which made her laugh.

Oh, she was in a really good mood today!

Unfortunately, Jackson wasn't there. She had hoped he would be in already, prepping for his day, but the kitchen was empty. Not thinking Jackson or anybody else would mind, Stevie put on a pot of coffee. Then she retrieved the cake from the walk-in, placed it on the big stainless-steel counter, found the ingredients she needed for the buttercream icing and layers of raspberry and cream filling—all of which she'd already arranged to pay Jackson for—and got to work.

The white cake was one of Alissa's favorites, and Stevie had made it many times. Yet, she was still relieved when the layers for the two tiers came together beautifully. She placed her creation on a round dove gray platter and iced it with the softest hue of dusty blue she'd ever managed to blend. When she had the smooth finish she desired, she wrapped each tier in transparent edible lace ribbon and wound a string of realistic-looking edible pearls around each layer. Finally, she carefully arranged white camellias, silver leaves, and tiny pinecones with dusty blue berries on the wide ledge of the bottom tier.

When she nestled the joyful Alissa and Jed miniatures into a spot beside the spill of flowers, her breath hitched in her throat. "Let them be happy," she whispered ferociously under her breath. "Please."

Standing back, she studied her work critically. Then smiled. Alissa would like it a lot, she was pretty sure.

Placing the decorated cake in a box and stashing it in the cooler, she cleaned up, leaving no trace she'd even been in the kitchen. Then she pulled out her phone and texted, "Cake done. I honestly thought you'd be here." She added a smiley face and hit send.

Then typed again. "HOPED, I mean."

"Me too," came the reply. "Got tied up with—ugh."

That's curious, Stevie thought, but before she could ponder Jackson's words too deeply, her phone pinged again. "Will explain later. Have fun today. Text when you're free, no matter how late."

"Will do," Stevie typed—then added two kisses for good measure. "XX."

Jackson's response whizzed back through the ether instantly. "Not fair. I want those in person."

Stevie grinned as she locked up and made her way out of the kitchen. She'd decorated the cake in record time, and it was still early. If she hurried, she'd have time for a much-needed soak in Jo's suite before heading to Alissa's room for a hair and makeup session.

Making her way down the long hallway to Jo's suite, her dress carefully wrapped in plastic, draped over one arm, her shoes, undergarments, and cosmetics in a bag over her shoulder, Stevie wondered if she should text Jo to give her a heads up. But then thought, nah. Doing so would mean finding somewhere to lie her dress down so she could rummage in her bag for her phone. Besides, they'd already discussed her taking a shower in Jo's hotel room before getting ready for the wedding. Jo wouldn't care that she was showing up earlier than planned in the hope she could soak in a bathtub—the luxury!—instead.

Hoping to sneak in without waking Jo if she was lucky enough to be sleeping in, Stevie used the room card Jo had given her earlier in the week. There was click and whirr as the door unlocked. She opened the door, slipped inside—then froze in the entranceway, gawking. What the heck? Had she gotten the wrong room? But if that was the case, why did her key work?

But no—there was Jo rushing toward her. Stevie's head

swung toward the kitchen again. And yep, the handsome guy making coffee was still there. She had a strange feeling of déjà vu, but at the same time, he was real. Definitely not a figment of her overactive imagination. Jo had a man in her room! And Stevie had . . . blundered in.

She found her voice and shook her head. "Sorry." Then she raised a teasing eyebrow at Jo. "I guess I should have called first."

Jo blushed—a rare thing for her. She usually had such a good poker face. "No, it's not a problem. We just fell asleep watching movies until early this morning."

"Uh-huh." Stevie nodded, then turned her back on the man, so she could give Jo a big wink without him seeing.

Jo rolled her eyes, and Stevie barely managed to hold back a giggle. She waved her shower bag and wedding accouterments in explanation. "I just came to grab a quick soak and start getting ready for the ceremony. We're supposed to meet in Alissa's room to get all gussied up."

"Right, right," Jo's head bobbed. "You go ahead. Bathroom's all yours."

Stevie was headed toward Jo's bedroom when she spotted a gorgeous golden retriever. He lifted his head off his paws and looked happy to see her. She gave his silky ears a good rub, then grinned at Jo. "I see how it is. One's not enough, hey? You have to keep *two* handsome guys penned up with you?"

She scooted into the luxurious bathroom and managed to shut the door before Jo could playfully swat her.

When Stevie emerged from the tub, gloriously overheated and loose feeling, the man was gone, and Jo offered her a decadent huckleberry scone from Mabel's—a Granite Ridge treasure. She closed her eyes, savoring the first bite—then had a thought that made her eyes flash open.

"Is this a bribe?" she mumbled through her mouthful.

"Whatever could you mean?" Jo asked innocently, then

whisked the plate holding the sumptuous treat away. "Of course, if you want to taste this again, you'll never tell another soul you saw Luke here."

"Oh, *Luke*, is it—wait!" The nagging feeling that the man was somehow familiar, which Stevie had ignored in the confusion of the moment, suddenly made sense. Years fell off the man she'd seen filling the coffee pot with water, and her mind's eye showed the baby-faced, lanky adolescent he'd been. "Of course! Your best of besties in your childhood library haunting days."

Jo didn't confirm or deny, just smiled happily.

"Of course, I won't tell anyone. It's your news to share. Now give me that plate."

Jo laughed and handed the scone-laden saucer back. "I would've let you have it anyway."

"I know." Stevie took another bite, but the buttery treat seemed dry now in light of the thoughts racing through her. "Are you serious about Luke? Are you going to let yourself fall in love with him?"

At first, Jo looked affronted. "Why would you ask that? It's a little soon for talk of love," she said sternly, but then her tone softened as she realized Stevie wasn't teasing—or criticizing. She was serious. "But maybe . . . I don't know. Why?"

In a rush, knowing she'd better blab fast or she'd lose her nerve, Stevie confessed how drawn she was to Jackson—still, with absolutely no less intensity, despite all the years that had passed. Then, hardly able to squeeze the words out, she revealed what was holding her back from unreservedly hoping big and going all out for him. "What if I'm like my mother—unable to commit, unable to love for whatever reasons, not stable enough to have a family of my own? Then there's the whole living in an RV, not really having a steady job thing. Not many people look upon a transient lifestyle as favorable."

For a long, heavy moment, Jo didn't say anything. The

furrow on her brow and the intense look in her eyes said she had plenty of thoughts, however. She was just figuring out how best to articulate them. Finally, she took Stevie's hand.

"You are not your biological mother."

Jo went on to say a whole lot of other nice things, like how strong she thought Stevie was, how loyal, how protective, etc., etc. Then Jo reminded Stevie of how Maddie had given them the gift—and the stellar example—of choosing love, choosing happiness, and stitching together a devoted family out of what so many others had cast aside and deemed to have no value.

"We deserve to be loved and to love," she finished, her strong voice ringing with authority and wisdom.

Stevie could suddenly see how Jo must be in court, and she wanted to believe she knew what she was talking about. She really did. But you couldn't cook as much as she did and not know that quality ingredients turned out quality dishes, and mediocre ones created second-rate fare. People were more complex (arguably!) than food products, but there was a still a broadly applicable truth in her observation.

"You're so wise, Jo." Stevie finally managed, fully meaning it, even while fully knowing that it still wasn't so simple. Jo had experienced hard things too, and to an outsider, maybe they'd appear the same, but Stevie knew better. Jo came from good stock. The people who loved her hadn't left her; they'd been taken from her. Stevie, on the other hand? Well, enough said. She couldn't be more different than Jo in every way that counted. Still, Stevie had done a lot of work on herself over the years and knew she was her own worst critic. If Jo saw the qualities she said she did in Stevie— and believed that Marilyn's flaws weren't imprinted on her DNA—maybe, just maybe she was right. She'd consider the possibility anyway.

"As usual, you've given me lots to think about. Thank you. I'm so lucky to have you for a sister."

"You give me too much credit," Jo said with her customary humility.

"No, I don't."

They were both quiet a moment, then Jo, ever practical, got to her feet. "We'd better get this show on the road."

"Agreed," Stevie said, following her lead and getting ready to head out of the hotel room. But she couldn't just leave after such a conversation, without saying or doing something to show Jo what she meant to her.

"What's Luke's favorite snack?" Stevie asked, then continued before Jo got a word in edgewise, "Never mind! I know the perfect thing. I'll make you guys a sexy sampler of goodies and leave them in your fridge. They'll keep well, so you can just have them whenever the mood hits this week."

Jo gave Stevie a fond, knowing look. "I love you too, sis."

CHAPTER 14

The wedding was as beautiful as Stevie had known it would be, all soft blues and grays and natural accents, wintery and romantic in every way. And yet, all the tiny, carefully chosen details, pretty as they were, hardly mattered. Jed and Alissa could've gotten married in a barren wasteland, her in a gunny sack, him in a barrel, and they would've elicited the same awed sighs and happy tears from everyone who witnessed them.

Alissa was already a beauty, inside and out—and no, Stevie wasn't just a biased big sister. Today, however, with joy radiating from her whole being as her eyes lit on Jed and she walked down the aisle to officially begin the rest of their life together, she was an absolute stunner. And the expression on Jed's face, so filled with love and awe that you couldn't possibly miss it, went a long way to softening Stevie's concerns. You could fake a lot of things, but it was hard to manufacture the kind of tenderness his gaze carried. And Stevie was further encouraged by the fact that when he misted up, he didn't seem embarrassed or try to hide it. And when Alissa reached him and stretched up on tiptoes to gently wipe an escaped tear from his cheek, there wasn't a dry eye in the place.

Stevie had also been mulling over the things he'd said during his formal apology. She, of all people, knew the powerful effect a toxic family member could have on a person —and if Alissa could see past his failings, forgive him and give Jed another chance, surely, she could extend similar grace. Even if it pissed her off a little to do so.

And then, practically in a blink, the ceremony was over. Alissa was Mrs. Marsh, and everyone was hugging and greeting the new married couple and offering best wishes. When it was Stevie's turn in the informal greeting line, she hugged Alissa without words. If Alissa was surprised by the spontaneous gesture on Stevie's behalf, she didn't show it. And then Stevie was standing in front of Jed.

"Stevie," he said.

"Jed."

"I love your sister. I won't let her—or any of you—down again. I promise."

A slight movement made Stevie look down, and she realized Alissa had grabbed her new husband's hand and squeezed it. The solidarity in the gesture made Stevie smile and emphasized, again, Alissa's faith in Jed. Stevie decided to believe in him too. Mostly, of course, for her little sister—but also for herself. She needed there to be love in the world— and for there to be relationships between men and women that worked out. Everyone did.

"I know you do," she said softly, then added, "welcome back, bro. We missed you."

Jed bear-hugged Stevie, and she let him because, well, it was a wedding, after all.

"Thank you," Alissa said, hugging Stevie too. "Things got complicated between us because of Jed's family stuff. I didn't handle it well, but we made it through. Together."

Stevie squeezed Alissa back.

❄

"I wish I could've danced with you tonight," Jackson said, his eyes riveted on the removal of her jacket, the reveal of her dress. They were, surprise, surprise, standing in Jackson's pub's busy kitchen.

Stevie was dusted with a smattering of regret. Maybe she shouldn't have been such a coward and should've invited him to the wedding.

And yet, knowing what she knew—that no matter how much he said otherwise, this "seeing where it went" experiment would end, regardless of how much she wished differently—she couldn't bear to be seen "officially dating" Jackson by her family, then having to tell them when it, when *she*, failed again. They'd be so kind, so supportive. It would shred her.

Jackson played with the fabric of her sleeve, and his eyes darkened, and his voice roughened. "This dress on you is . . . wow. Is it this soft . . . all over?"

Stevie laughed. "Has a line like that *ever* worked for you?"

Jackson winked. "I'll find out any second now and let you know."

"Har har." But the idea of letting him find out, the thought of his hands caressing the length of her body beneath that soft, slippery fabric, did funny things to her insides and made her suck in a breath.

Jackson glanced over his shoulder to see how close any of the kitchen staff were, then leaned in. "The kitchen's closing in half an hour, and Val can muddle through, no problem. I already told everyone I might duck out early, so while the last thing I want you to do is to cover up . . . "

He held out her jacket to help her back into it.

"Great," she said as her coat glided over her arms. "Where should we go?"

"How does my condo sound?"

Her insides fluttered.

"Or, if you're not comfortable hanging out there—"

"No, it's great, but I hardly slept last night and tomorrow's Christmas. I don't want to be an overtired nightmare for my family's morning together, so don't let me stay super late. Even if I change my mind and beg, don't let me. Promise."

Jackson laughed, then raised his hand like he was swearing an oath. "Before you turn into a pumpkin at midnight, whether you're ready to go or not, it'll be out into the snow with you."

He took her hand as they walked, and it felt like both the most comfortable, natural thing in the world—and the sexiest, most thrilling novelty. The village streets were quiet, the restaurants and pubs already closed—or just about to, like Jackson's—as most people were enjoying Christmas Eve festivities with family and friends by now. The snow muted all sound, making the winter wonderland surrounding them feel like their own private refuge. Overhead a million stars shone down, so big and bright it felt like Stevie should be able to reach up and grab one to wish upon. And if she did, she knew exactly what she'd wish for. That all that was happening this magical week wasn't merely a dream fantasy on her part—that this time with Jackson was the start of something as real as it felt.

"What are you thinking about?" he asked as they stopped to look up at the village Christmas tree, a living pine festooned with thousands of lights, so perfectly shaped and huge that Stevie wondered if the lodge owners had purposefully built around it, envisioning this enchanting festive centerpiece.

"Just all this . . ." She motioned at the tree, the sky—*him*. "It's so nice it makes me feel extra sad that we—or, I guess, more honestly, *I*—blew us up before we ever got a chance to see if we'd work."

Jackson shook his head, and in the glow of the massive tree, his face was deadly serious. "No. We were kids—and pretty messed up ones. It couldn't have lasted—like we proved. This way, meeting now, as adults when we actually have a chance, is so much better."

As they moved away from the tree, turning a corner toward a row of posh condos, Stevie surprised herself by stating exactly what was on her neurotic mind. "You really think there's a possibility that this isn't just some little Christmas walk down memory lane for old time's sake?"

"I can't speak for you, obviously." He smiled. "But for me? I definitely already know I want us to be a lot more than a holiday fling."

What do you see in me that makes you so sure? she wanted to ask, but they were suddenly in Jackson's stone-tiled entranceway, and he was ushering her in. As he puttered in the galley kitchen, which was completely tricked out with stainless-steel everything and a gorgeous double-fridge, making them a snack, she was so busy taking in her surroundings, studying how Jackson lived, that her age-old insecurities shut up for a moment.

"So, what do you think of my digs?" he asked, handing her a mug of something hot and frothy that smelled deliciously of vanilla and bergamot. Even before her tongue touched the beverage's delicate layer of foam, Stevie was sure she was about to enjoy a London Fog.

"I know it's small, but—"

She laughed. "Small? You don't know small until you've seen my place."

"I can't wait. When you said you pretty much lived in the area, only leaving for stints of work, and that you own your own home . . . " His smile grew a little shy or self-conscious, and he sipped his tea. "Well, I was thrilled that you're this grounded person, comfortable in your own place, happy to maintain deep roots in your small town. All these years, I've been trying to pretend otherwise, but that's all I want too: to settle down in Granite Ridge and put down roots. Deep ones that are hopefully never uprooted again."

Stevie had been about to take another mouthful of tea. She'd been right. He'd made London Fogs, and they were beyond scrumptious. But now she paused, mug halfway to her lips, and stared. He'd obviously deeply misunderstood about her home, about her "roots," and about her being comfortable and content in one place.

And she'd misunderstood him equally as much. Given the bit he'd shared about all his various training jaunts and jobs all over the globe the past years, she'd thought they had that in common. Had started to imagine them gallivanting together.

"What?" he asked, sensing that he'd erred somehow.

"Um, you know my home is an RV, right?"

"Yeah, that's some brand of a modular home or tiny house, right?"

"Uh, no. An RV—like a motorhome. Actually, not even 'like a motorhome.' An *actual* motorhome. I live in a vintage Toyota Sunrader that I did most of the renovations on personally. It's got a generator, solar panels, water—" She stopped talking, realizing he was still struggling with the original part of her sentence and wouldn't care one bit that she was equipped to live off-grid. She chuckled but didn't feel mirthful exactly. Leave it to Jackson Bassett to not know what an RV was! Well, he did, obviously, just living in a motorhome was such a foreign concept that his brain hadn't put it together. It sort of made sense. He and his dad flew to Europe most summers and to somewhere hot and tropical most winters. He'd probably never been in a camper or camping trailer in his life.

He didn't say anything, so she added, "Wait till you see it. You'll love it. It's super cozy." And her home really was cozy. And upbeat and funky. And practical. And on that thought, something struck her. When Jackson asked what she thought of his "digs" earlier and she hadn't answered, it was because she was trying to pick up some, any, vibe of him in the place. She hadn't been able to, until he'd given her the delicious tea, anyway. The sweet beverage was all Jackson, but the condo, though sleek and polished and appealing in a dark glossy wood, granite, and charcoal gray décor sort of way, looked put together by someone else, for a generic anybody. For a guy who wanted a "home," his place was anything but. And never mind a Christmas tree. He didn't have a single Christmas ornament hanging anywhere!

Jackson still hadn't spoken, and she realized something else. He wasn't mute out of embarrassment for not getting the whole RV concept. He looked . . . horrified for her. Her hackles rose a little. It was one thing for her to have an inferiority complex from time to time, but it was another thing altogether for someone else to view her or her life as inferior, especially someone who claimed to like her and think she was "so great."

"I'm not living in a dumpster, pulling a shopping cart I jacked from a grocery store or anything. It's super nice."

"But it's so . . . transient."

Stevie's eyebrows rose, but her stomach plummeted. He'd used the very word she had when voicing her concerns to Jo, the word she hated. "Uh, yeah, because hello, I *am* transient. Something you should've picked up on when we were swapping bios and sharing what we were up to the last decade."

He shook his head, looking gobsmacked. "I'm sorry. I guess I heard all that through my own experiences. I thought it paled for you, the way it had for me. All I ever wanted was one home in one town. I hated being shuffled all over the globe for my dad's work—and the two and a half years I spent in Granite Ridge, where I met you, were the best years of my life. When I realized I was reliving—and still hating—the exact life I swore I'd never have, I headed back here, with plans to stay. That's why the changes regarding the pub have hit me so hard. I need to figure out a new restaurant and find a new location. I thought you had a similar epiphany about planting yourself permanently, and that yeah, you bought an RV." He blushed. "I really thought it was just a brand I hadn't heard of."

Stevie set her half-finished tea down on a glass-topped metal coffee table. "It's so sad." She meant it. It really was. "It's like we have mirror issues but did the exact opposite with them. I want a home—and when you see it, you'll get it —it is my home. But I never want to get attached to one solitary place again, rely on someone else to provide my house, or to be dependent on someone else for that feeling of home. I have to know that if I ever need to, I can pick up and go, just like that—and that nothing, nobody, has the power to yank my home out from under me ever again."

"Wow . . ." Jackson shook his head, sounding dazed. "We really do have different goals."

Stevie nodded, then winced. "Do you want me to go?"

Did she imagine a slight hesitation before he said, "No, no, of course not. We're still . . . seeing where we end up, right?"

Just as Stevie said, "Right. Good," a timer rang in the kitchen.

Jackson disappeared for a moment, then reappeared, bearing a platter of garlic baked brie and sides of pecans and crostini to scoop the cheese onto. A little dish of cranberry preserves promised to be the perfect sweet compliment to the savory deliciousness.

They ended up having a nice enough evening, making small talk while they prepped dishes for a Christmas potluck dinner Jackson was attending at a friend's house in Granite Ridge the next day, but Stevie wasn't kidding herself. "Nice enough" was a total letdown after her spicy daydreams about a Christmas Eve spent cuddled up with Jackson in front of a crackling fire—and maybe some follow up kisses that would put their recent one to shame.

No, despite Jackson's words to the contrary, discovering their dreams for the future were different had cooled his interest in her just as quickly as her tea chilled on the cold glass table.

At eleven-thirty, she readied herself to leave—and insisted he didn't need to accompany her. He argued but eventually gave in. At the door, he touched her hair and smiled down at her, somewhat sadly, she thought. Still, she half expected him to kiss her, even lifted her face like an idiot—but no kiss came. Instead, he stepped back somewhat awkwardly. Her cheeks burned.

"I guess that's a night then," he said softly, then checked his wristwatch—some huge expensive thing that was totally impractical for kitchen work. "I'll probably drink too much tomorrow and end up crashing on my friend's couch, and will most likely stay over Boxing Day too, so I'd better say it now . . . Merry Christmas in twenty-five minutes."

"Uh, yeah, to you too," she mumbled, completely confused at how their evening, not fantastic but not cringingly awful, had devolved so quickly. She couldn't get out the door fast enough.

A cold wind had kicked up again, blowing snowflakes that felt like small crystal blades into her flushed face. It was a welcome distraction—and cooling agent—as she quickly made her way back to her "transient" home.

CHAPTER 15

S tevie awoke to the softly tinkling alarm she'd set the night before—"I Heard the Bells on Christmas Day"— which grew louder in tiny increments until she clicked it off. She stretched to flick the switch by the edge of her bed, and her little Christmas tree and the cheery string of lights she'd strung twinkled into merry life.

Despite her disappointment with how the previous night with Jackson had gone—as in it hadn't gone anywhere, and they seemed less connected than ever, petering out before they'd even begun—her stomach jumped with happy excitement. She couldn't help it. With a passion equaling how much she'd hated Christmas the first twelve or so years of her life, she now loved it—and had for the past fifteen years. It marked the anniversary of her family. And this year wouldn't disappoint. Even with the wedding festivities on, then off, then on again, one plan had never been called into question: their Christmas Day brunch. It would be held in Maddie's luxurious suite and was being catered, plus old married-lady Alissa wasn't coming out of her honeymoon cabin for anything, not even Christmas with her sisters, so it would definitely have a different feel than other years, but that didn't matter. What made the season special was them all being together—in spirit, if not in body. Change and growth were inevitable, after all, even exciting. Why not embrace them?

Stevie's brain fizzed at her own thought. Change and growth were *what*? Embrace *what*? Who was she? She grinned. Apparently, she could rest easy; she'd been telling the truth when she'd told Jackson she'd grown a lot since their old days.

Everyone seemed thrilled by the gifts she'd made them— jars of herb-infused bath salts and beautiful boxes of home-made fudge. And she felt like a giddy eight-year-old about hers, just some of which included a cheery pair of flower print cooking clogs from Jo, a fun luxury that, although prac-tical, she wouldn't have treated herself to, hilariously awesome green and white striped pajamas with red trim from Maddie, as per the new jammies at Christmas tradition, and a book from Hailey that was "too good" to not own in paper-back, despite their shared love of eBooks, along with a cozy wrap.

All in all, it was a lovely morning, but over too quickly. After discovering Luke in Jo's suite, Stevie suspected Jo might duck out. But Maddie and Hailey also had plans? That was a surprise—though not the biggest one of the day. Not by far.

Weighed down with her Christmas loot and looking forward to spending Christmas afternoon curled up in bed reading (Genuinely! She wasn't pining for Jackson. *She wasn't.*), Stevie almost didn't bother to check her phone when it vibrated in her hip pocket.

She changed her mind before heading out the lobby doors, however, in case it was Maddie or Hailey deciding they wanted company, after all. It was a good thing she checked. It was Jackson, and his message was cryptic.

"Last night wasn't what I envisioned for us. I need to explain myself. I know you're busy with your family today though, and it felt wrong to try to insert myself or cancel on my friends. But one thing can't wait. GO TO THE FRONT DESK AS SOON AS POSSIBLE."

His use of ALL CAPS was confusing, stressful even, and Stevie found herself practically sprinting to the counter.

There was no one around except for two desk clerks, one of whom was cuddling an incredibly cute bristle brush of a dog against her chest, while the other stroked its incongruously silky ears, crooning silly—and entirely true—endearments to it. If the little dog hadn't brought a smile to her face, the shiny red satin bow around his neck, almost as big as he was, certainly would have.

Definitely a terrier mutt of some kind, Stevie thought, and her heart panged as Ed's dear face sprang into her mind.

The dog-holding clerk noticed her. "Oh, I'm so sorry, ma'am. I didn't see you walk up."

"I don't blame you. He's adorable."

"Isn't he just? And he's a Christmas present—" The clerk grew flustered suddenly. "I'm sorry," she repeated, giving Stevie a strange evaluating look. "How can I help you?"

"I'm Stevie Fox. I was told—"

The woman nearly dropped the small dog in her hurry to put him back in a large silver striped box, which contained a small food dish, an "unspillable" water bowl, and a fluffy gray blanket. "He was perfectly happy in his cozy little box, but he's so cute. We didn't think you'd mind—"

"Of course not." Stevie grinned. "I wouldn't be able to resist either. But I'm here because—" She trailed off midsentence, staring uncomprehendingly at the scene unfolding in front of her.

All smiles, the other clerk placed a screened lid on the box and gently lifted it up onto the counter in front of Stevie. "Merry Christmas! Are you surprised?"

"I, um, don't understand. . . ." Stevie didn't lay a finger on the box, which shuffled and rustled as the dog play-wrestled with the blanket. All of a sudden, he paused, cocked his head, and looked directly up at her as if to say, "What are you waiting for?"

"He's yours!" said the first clerk.

"It's such a romantic present!" The second clerk reached for a soft blue envelope. "He gave you this too."

"Who did? I'm confused."

For the first time, the clerks looked a little less than rapturously delighted with themselves. "Jackson Bassett? He dropped this—and the dog off for you—for Christmas?"

Jackson got her a dog for Christmas? What a ridiculously irresponsible thing for him to do. It was the worst thing to get someone for Christmas. And yet, taking in the little dog's black button of a nose and meeting its chocolate brown eyes, which shone with intelligence and wit, Stevie's heart melted.

Still, first things first, she'd better read whatever the card said before she committed to taking the dog with her. The card—not a Christmas card, per se, but a replica of a vintage card with a picture of a black, curly-haired dog in the window of a pet shop—was packed with words on both sides.

Merry Christmas, Stevie, and surprise! (A good one, I hope!) As soon as I heard about this one-year-old fella, who needed to be rehomed, then saw his picture, I knew he was your dog. (If you disagree, I'm fully prepared to keep him myself, so please don't think I'm terribly irresponsible. Normally, I would never give an animal as a gift.)

His words so closely matched Stevie's exact initial response that she laughed out loud. The two clerks, probably starting to worry they were going to have the dog on their hands all shift—which no doubt made him a lot less cute—smiled nervously.

I know you're still mourning and feeling gun shy, so I hope it's not too soon—but from how you described Ed, he sounds like the enthusiastic sort of chap who understood we have to grab every chance for happiness and pleasure in this short life, even if it means risking the possibility of hurt.

I also hope that with this new guy in your life for company, kisses, long walks, and a constant appetite for snacks, you'll still have room and desire to keep me around.

Love,

Jackson

P.S. If you don't want him, if you can at least watch him for me until tomorrow, that would be awesome. If that doesn't work for you either, I'll really feel like a tool, but just text me. I have alternative arrangements if necessary.

The dog whined, then yipped—very quietly.

Stevie leaned her face close to the screen lid and whispered, "Oh, good boy! You already have an indoor voice." All she wanted to do was scoop the dog out and cuddle him right away, but then she feared she'd never discipline herself to put him back in the box. "Come, my friend. Let's go home."

The clerks both looked a little misty-eyed as Stevie thanked them, misty-eyed herself, for taking care of her surprise and wished them a very, very Merry Christmas.

Her heart was full as she spent the day alone, snuggling Syd while she read, taking him on multiple walks (Ed's sweet little down-filled vest with the fur-trimmed hood fit him perfectly, making her doubly happy she'd kept it), and sending her sisters and Maddie so many pictures of her new buddy that they were no doubt exasperated, though, to their credit, never said as much, only expressed delight for her. "I'm so happy for you," Jo texted, along with a string of hearts and dog emojis. "I know how lonely you've been since dear Ed died."

It was funny how expectations worked, Stevie thought as her quiet day wound down. Yesterday, which she'd had such high hopes for, had disappointed. Today, which, after brunch was over, she'd totally thought would be kind of dismal was . . . perfect. It didn't escape her that Jackson was the root cause of both. She wondered if the dog was a weird sort of consolation present—something Jackson would use to comfort himself for cutting her loose after she'd admitted how lonely she was. *I didn't leave her lonelier than ever. I gave her a dog—woman's best friend.*

Or maybe the dog was a fledgling step toward her and Jackson building a life together, regardless of how differently they saw the future. The end of his note seemed to suggest that.

Still, she had resisted texting him anything more than a quick thank you message during the day, confirming she'd gotten his "gift" and that yes, she planned to keep the little dog. She knew he'd be busy with his friends and didn't want him reading her texts when he was distracted. Now, however, with Syd tucked in for the night, seeming for all the world like he'd lived with her for years, she climbed into bed too—wearing her new Christmas PJs—and sent Jackson a good night wish.

"Yesterday was fine, but "fine" felt . . . disappointing. It was like we both had unspoken things between us. Today it was like our hearts matched. Like even though we've been separated by all these years and time, you still truly know me—and knew exactly what I needed. I can't even tell you how much I love Syd already. As you noted, he DOES feel meant for me. Thank you so much. Merry Christmas. Drive safe. Xoxoxoxox."

So, it was a bit mushy. If you couldn't be mushy at Christmas, when could you be? And if the dog was meant to be a consolation present . . . well, at least it really was a consoling one—and she'd stand by the sentiments she'd sent Jackson, regardless.

CHAPTER 16

The overnight parking area had been quiet all week, but even so, when Stevie first stirred to consciousness, the quality of the deep, deep silence startled her. She could hear . . . absolutely nothing. Not a sound. Her eyes flashed open—and the light was . . . strange. Bright but oddly gray somehow. What the—

Syd sensed she was awake in that way pets do, even though she hadn't moved anything but her eyelids. He bounced up with instant happy, hyper-alertness, bounding over to her from where he'd been curled—the foot of her bed.

She laughed, sat up, and pulled him into her lap. "You little scamp! Ed's bed isn't good enough for you?"

He shook his head, then cocked an ear.

She laughed again. "Clever boy already speaks human. Want to go for a pee?"

He bounced again—probably a coincidence, but still pretty hilarious.

She slid a coat on over her PJs, pulled on boots, and clipped a lead onto Syd's sparkly blue and rhinestone collar. Whoever owned him before her definitely shared her and Ed's taste in dog accessories!

When she unlocked the door and pushed to open it, she met resistance. She pushed harder. There was the sensation of shoving against a great weight. Then, with a crash of snow from overhead and a blast of icy powder in her face, the door finally opened.

The world that greeted her and Syd was a blur of feature-less white. The thick silence and weird quality of the light suddenly made sense: it had snowed in the night—and what a snowfall. A smooth field of the white stuff had obliterated all evidence of the lodge's diligent snowplowing and path grooming. Snow lay in heavy folds on top of the other vehicles in the lot and cascaded down their sides. Between the snow from above and the equally thick layer rising from the ground, they were almost buried. There must be three feet of fresh snow!

Stevie opened the closet beside the door and retrieved a snow shovel—grateful she'd had the foresight to take the shovel inside for the winter, rather than leave it in its usual storage spot in an exterior compartment on the RV. It was awkward shoveling stairs off while standing above them, but she quickly got them cleared enough to descend. Then she made a three-foot clearing. Syd zipped down the stairs behind her, did his business, then bolted back to the snow-free zone of the motorhome.

"Wimp!" Stevie chuckled and wondered if she should dig a path—then opted for Syd's line of thinking. No doubt, the lodge would be going around with a plow truck or snow-blower soon. In the meantime, she'd enjoy her little snowed-in cocoon.

She'd just plugged in her Christmas lights and started a pot of coffee when there was a knock on her door. Expecting a worker from the lodge, she cracked the door an inch, Syd dancing around her feet.

Then she threw the door open wide.

"Jackson! You're the last person I was expecting."

"Well, that kind of makes me feel like a jerk," he said, but his eyes twinkled. "Hopefully, it's not a disappointment."

"Of course not. Come in, come in." She remembered then she was still in pajamas. She motioned down at herself. "I wasn't expecting company of any kind, obviously."

"You look like a sexy elf," Jackson said, his eyes warm, "but I admit I'm glad you weren't planning to entertain someone else wearing those."

"Well, except for Syd, of course."

"I meant to tell you I love the name Syd. It's perfect for him." Jackson reached down and rubbed Syd's silky ears, then grinned up at her. "I take it he's not going to be my dog then?"

It was on the tip of Stevie's tongue to say, "Not just yours, anyway," but she felt too shy. He'd expressed such contempt for her lifestyle. What came out was, "What are you doing here?

Jackson didn't answer right away. Instead, he motioned down at his snow-crusted legs. "Do you mind if I take these off before I come in?"

Stevie hadn't noticed what he was wearing, and now she laughed. "Aw, you're wearing snow pants. So cute! Yes, by all means, take 'em off if you're staying."

"Oh, I'm staying," he said, peeling them off and, at her direction, hanging them, along with his jacket, in the same closet where she kept the shovel and broom.

"Coffee?" she asked.

"Yes, please. It smells fantastic. But first . . ."

Stevie didn't have even a second to wonder what he meant by that. He pulled her into his arms, tilted her chin, and kissed her—lightly at first, but then, when she kissed back, like a starving man being offered his favorite meal.

When they broke apart, Stevie's knees were literally weak. "Well, that was a nice surprise," she said, voice a bit wobbly.

"Nice?" Jackson's eyes glinted. "I think it was more than . . . nice. A lot more, in fact."

He was right, of course.

"Oh, the ego on you," Stevie teased, finding refuge in humor the way she always did—trying to ignore the speed of her still-ramped heartbeat. "I think we'll have to have another go before I make that ruling."

"That can definitely be arranged." Jackson stepped closer again, eyes blazing. Stevie inhaled sharply. She wasn't complaining about this rapid change of heart—or heat— between them since their flat Christmas Eve visit, but she was confused by how rapidly—and completely—he had switched gears. He read her mind, and instead of kissing her again, he patted her cheek. "But it will have to wait a bit."

He took a seat, and she poured them coffee. "I'll happily give you all the evidence you need to pass a verdict on my kissing ability, but first . . . I need to apologize for how I acted on the twenty-fourth—and hopefully, this will be the last time you and I torture each other with our confusing hot then cold game."

Stevie settled in the seat across from him, then sipped her coffee, listening.

"I like you so much. Too much, even. It's freaking me out. I keep telling myself to take it slow. That we're not the lovesick kids we used to be. That we're likely not even the same people now that we were then, but it's not working. I feel exactly the same. I still want the exact same things. And you . . . you feel the same to me. I know we've hardly even hung out, but when we're together . . . it just feels right."

The sweet sentiment made her heart squeeze with joy and hope, but also . . . unease. "How does that fit the last time we were together, though? I wasn't pushing you away that night at your place. I . . . *showed up*. I was totally open to . . . you. To seeing, to quote you, where we'd go . . . and then you were all weird and standoffish just because I . . . what? Don't own my own mansion in Granite Ridge?"

"I was an ass," Jackson said simply. "I got scared. In my mind, I think I was already seeing us married and setting up house—"

Stevie inhaled like she was scalded. She wasn't really hearing this. He wasn't as nuts as she was, was he?

Jackson shot her a worried look like he'd blown his chance with her with that confession. "And hearing that you shared no such fantasy, that you've never wanted what I always have, made me want to protect myself. Not put myself out there."

Stevie could definitely relate to the last bits. The part she didn't know how to explain was that it wasn't that she never dreamed of settling down or of building a home with someone—with him, actually—it was that she'd never been able, thus far, to convince herself it could actually work out. What did she have to offer anyone long term?

"Say I felt even remotely similarly delusional . . . "

He smiled ruefully at her joke.

"Don't you think it's too soon for you, for me, for *us* to be feeling any of this—or at least to be saying it out loud?"

Jackson shrugged. "Not at all. Some of the best dishes take eons of time to prepare and get ready. Others are super quick but are equally amazing and endlessly satisfying."

Stevie wanted to trust the happy surge of wellbeing and rightness she experienced whenever she was with Jackson, but she knew better. "Feelings aren't reality. Infatuation doesn't last."

"I disagree. Feelings are real—some of them anyway, and love, especially. Love is real. And it can last. I know it can."

Stevie had no reply for that because, in her own family, at least . . . she'd seen it proven that he was right.

"So what changed?" she asked. "You were scared, wanted to protect yourself in case I didn't feel the same way or want the same things, but now all of a sudden, you're here, saying all this."

"Nothing's changed. I came to my senses, that's all. You're worth the risk. Having a chance for happiness with you, the girl—the woman—I never got over, outweighs the possibility of getting hurt."

"But why? What on earth do you—could you ever—see in me?" Stevie's heart hurt even as she asked it. It was such a pathetic, scraping question, but she had to know. "I'm nothing. I came from nothing. I have nothing. I'm a . . . nobody that not even her own mother could love."

Jackson's jaw tightened. He looked furious. "That is such bullshit. Of all the things I dislike about your birth mother, how she made you feel like this, made you unable to see yourself the way other people see you . . . It makes me mental!" He took an angry breath. "You're tough. Funny. Resilient. Loyal. And that's just for starters."

Stevie held up a hand. "You don't have to do this."

Jackson caught her hand and pressed it to his lips. "Apparently, I do. I'm going to get you to see yourself the way I see you if it's the last thing I do."

Syd, who'd patiently let them hash things out and ignore him, could resist his rightful place at the center of their universe no longer. He grabbed his leash, which Stevie had left hanging on the door, brought it over to her, then stood up on his hind legs, and danced around in a begging circle.

Jackson laughed. "Well, I guess I know what we're doing next."

"Braving the snow from the looks of His Majesty—but afterward, do you want to hang out for the day?"

"It's cute you even thought you had a chance of getting rid of me."

The day passed in a happy blur, and more than once, Stevie's mind boggled that it was actually happening. It wasn't just a happy dream. They walked Syd in a maze of narrow paths, snow-blown by the lodge employees to enable people to get around until they could plow the rest. And it looked like they'd been wise to obey Syd's heeding and walk him. Snow started falling again—heavily—on their way back to Stevie's.

"It's perfect weather for holing up and doing nothing," Jackson said, grinning up at the sky, then blinking as heavy flakes pelted his face and caught in his eyelashes.

"Absolutely," Stevie agreed, sticking out her tongue, trying to catch a flake.

They grinned at each other and beelined for the RV. They made brunch. They snuggled and kissed on Stevie's bed, and although they were practically panting with desire, they didn't go further because they weren't in a hurry. They had time—maybe a lifetime of it, though Stevie was astounded she was even thinking that was possible—and there was an intense pleasure in prolonging desire. They napped.

And later in the afternoon, curled up together on the two-seater couch across from the Christmas tree, paging through a new issue of *The Art of Eating* magazine that Maddie had stuffed in her stocking, Jackson looked up. "You're right, by the way. Your home here, this RV, does feel like a real home."

Stevie smiled. "Well, du-uh." But his words made her recall something Maddie told her and her sisters multiple times as they were growing up. "Home isn't a building or a place. It's who you're with, who you love, and who loves you."

Stevie had liked the saying but hadn't always agreed . . . thought it was a sweet idea but maybe too simple. Now, however, she saw its profound truth. Being with Jackson, even—or maybe especially—when doing "nothing big," felt the same as being with her sisters and Maddie. Safe. Real. Dependable.

Of course, one thing was different . . . how crazy sexy Jackson was. Could you have safe and sexy and thrilling at the same time? She wanted to believe it.

"What's making you smile that smile?" Jackson asked, then poked her ribs playfully, knowing she was ticklish. She squirmed in his arms and yelped, "I'll never tell."

This led, of course, to some playful wrestling which led to more kissing . . .

Sometime later, Jackson—gratifyingly as breathless as she was—turned his attention from her to the little Christmas tree. "It's so cool that you put up a tree even though you live alone. I don't know why I've never thought to."

She grinned and tapped his head, then made a face. "Just as I suspected. Hollow. Good thing you're pretty."

"Not as pretty as you—"

"Don't start," she said, but inside she thought, Don't ever stop. Please.

"Your decorations are awesome. Do they have special significance?"

She nodded. "Yeah, actually. Every single one does."

He pointed to a delicate blown glass creation of four female-shaped figures that looked vaguely ghostlike.

"Oh, that's easy . . . Jo found that. We thought ghosts as a Christmas decoration was too cool. It's us, of course, the soul sisters."

Jackson smiled and pointed at a tiny pasta angel with a penne body, bowtie noodle wings, and macaroni arms holding a small paper songbook—all spray painted white and covered with gold glitter.

"One of Hailey's inventions when she was ten or eleven."

A tiny ceramic cactus in an equally tiny ceramic pot decorated with red ribbons and gold bells caught Jackson's attention next, and Stevie laughed out loud.

"Okay, you have to tell me the story behind that one if it makes you laugh like that."

Stevie did, sharing how one Christmas Alissa had gotten them each funky little plant decorations based on their personality types. Nan Claire got a mini ceramic prayer plant. Jo received a classic—and classy—ivy. I got . . . well, you can see for yourself."

Jackson chuckled. "I can see why she thought it fit, although she must know as well as I do that you're a softy under all those prickles—still, in general, it's right."

"Oh yeah?"

"Definitely." Jackson took her hand, pressed his lips to her wrist, then kissed a trail up to the hollow of her elbow. "A cactus is just a succulent, after all, and you're very . . . succulent."

Stevie wanted to laugh, but she was too mesmerized by the sensation of his mouth on her skin.

The evening wrapped up with popcorn and a movie— Disney's "The Fox and The Hound." Stevie had forgotten how much they both loved that one until Jackson, spotting it in her small collection of movies, beamed up at her and exclaimed, "Fox!"

Instantly, she remembered how she used to call him "Hound" because of his last name. How on earth had she ever forgotten that? Stevie was sure she wasn't imagining it: Syd was as delighted by the movie choice—and their little trio—as she was.

CHAPTER 17

S tevie woke—her head resting on one of Jackson's outstretched arms—aflutter with a delicious, slightly tipsy sense of disorientation. She was dreaming. She had to be—but no. Jackson—splayed on his back, still deep in sleep—was . . . here. With her. His gorgeous jaw, in need of a shave—or not—was right there. She pressed a kiss just below his ear and was rewarded with a sleepy smile.

"Hey there," he said, bending the arm beneath her to pull her close. At some point in the night, he'd stripped to his boxers and a soft T-shirt. She loved the warm sleepy, clean musk of him and wanted to rub up and down him like a cat. She settled for resting her chin on his chest and smiling up at him. "Hey yourself."

Syd, feeling the love, jumped from his spot on the bed—landing square on Jackson's T-shirted abs. "Ooof," Jackson said, sounding like a cartoon character. Stevie giggled.

She was about to offer coffee when Jackson's phone buzzed. He picked it up, read a message, and the happy, soporific look on his face disappeared.

"What's wrong?"

"Nothing . . . just not how I wanted to spend the day. I wanted to spend it with you."

Stevie smiled.

"But Val has flaked again. I need to go in and cover for her."

"Want help?" Stevie asked, wondering yet again about the state of Jackson's business. If this, if *they*, were really turning into a . . . thing—her heart jumped happily just thinking it—they'd have to talk about his pub sometime. But not right this minute.

"Really?"

"Of course—after all, I was hoping to spend the day with you too."

"That'd be awesome."

And it was. How could working with someone be as fun as spending leisure time with them? But somehow, that's exactly how it was for her and Jackson. She loved their rhythm in the kitchen. She admired his speed and dexterity—and at one point got a little caught up imagining him using those hands in more intimate ways than he had so far in their reunion . . . soon. Anticipation made her shiver.

"What?" he said like she'd spoken aloud.

"Aw, nothing." She grinned. "Just kitchen work is pretty sensual stuff, you know."

He laughed appreciatively, then growled, "I'll say," and pushed her up against one of the stainless-steel counters, kissing her passionately. Mostly they controlled themselves though—because there weren't enough times when they were alone in the kitchen to truly let themselves go. Probably a good thing—if delightfully frustrating.

At Jackson's prodding, Stevie took off for a few hours after the lunch rush to spend time with Syd and decided to take him to visit Nan. She hadn't gotten to see enough of her this holiday, and she knew being laid up with a sore back was driving her feisty, go-getter Nan crazy. Then she popped by

Jo's suite, knowing her dog-loving sister would adore her new dog nephew. Syd was beside himself with Jo's pampering attention, and his showboating for treats kept them laughing. Stevie hoped Jo would take the plunge one day—get her own dog, take a chance on love. She deserved it.

And what about you? her inner voice whispered. Maybe you do too.

Come to think of it, Stevie thought on her way back to drop Syd off at home before returning to Jackson's pub and the Karaoke night, her sisters and Maddie all seemed to be glowing lately—not just Alissa. She knew Jo's secret, of course, and suspected Hailey and Nick were becoming an item. Was there romance afoot in Maddie's life too?

No, what were the odds of that? That they'd all find love the same week in the same place? She was silly and love-struck and smitten—and was projecting the same onto her family. It, *she*, was ridiculous. The thought made her smile, scoop Syd up, and plant a kiss on his nose. She hoped her ridiculous state lasted forever! There, she admitted it—and that was the only smudge on the brightness of her day.

She wanted whatever this was between her and Jackson to last forever—but it was inevitably coming to an end. She and her family only had a few more days at Cedar Mountain Lodge. What would become of her and Jackson then? From the sounds of it, he'd be busy trying to get a new restaurant off the ground. Meanwhile, she'd already taken more weeks off in a row than she liked and had been putting out feelers for the spring season in some of the fishing lodges in BC. He'd been crystal clear that the idea of traveling around for work no longer appealed to him.

"Don't think about it," she commanded herself, then gave Syd another kiss and settled him in the RV. "Just enjoy what you guys have for now."

"You're worth it." Jackson's sweet words came back to her. He'd been talking about risking pain . . . but could he also have been saying she was worth the hassle of trying to make their very different lifestyles somehow fit together?

The ferocious hope that welled up in her at the thought was almost too much to bear—beautiful and excruciating, all at once.

When they were over, couldn't make it work—or wouldn't—she was going to be crushed. But for now? She would enjoy every moment with Jackson like she really could have him forever.

CHAPTER 18

S tevie woke early, almost as bouncy with enthusiasm for the new day as Syd. Jackson wasn't scheduled to go into work until much later in the day, and Stevie was looking forward to being a tourist—a tourist with a partner! The past few days with Jackson had spoiled her. There were things to be said about exploring a new place on your own—no arguments about what activities to go to, what sights to see, where to eat and when . . . but it was so fun to share experiences with someone else.

She checked the time. Too early to call without looking like the psycho she was. She took Syd out, showered and dressed, then lifted the blinds over the kitchen sink's window. The heavy snow of the past two days had stopped, the lodge had all the walkways and public areas groomed and beautiful, and bright lemon-yellow sunshine kissed everything with sparkles. They were planning to walk Cedar trail, whose views Jackson promised would "blow her mind," then have a "couple massage." That was a bit intimidating actually but in a yummy kind of way. Finally, they'd enjoy a soak in a hot tub, followed by an early dinner out before he went back to the pub for the Karaoke rush.

Her phone rang. Assuming it was Jackson, as eager for another day together as she was, she practically sang her "Hello!"

"Hello? Stevie?" said a low, craggy voice.

Dammit. Marilyn. Again. That was two calls in less than a week. Two calls *a year* was more her usual. She couldn't have burned through the money Stevie sent already, could she have? She kicked herself for not checking her phone's call display before answering and steeled herself.

"Hey, Mom."

"I was wondering if you could help me out?" Marilyn's voice cracked, and even though she was calling for another favor, the only reason she ever called, really, there was something different in her tone, something Stevie didn't recognize.

"I'm moving out, leaving Hank."

She was leaving someone—well, someone other than Stevie? Leaving a *man*? This was new. "I thought it was your apartment."

"Yeah, but . . . this is . . . better. Easier."

Easier for her to get out than to make him get out, she meant. Stevie sighed.

"I still have most of the money you gave me."

"Let me guess. You need more?"

"No." Marilyn didn't sound affronted or surprised by the accusation in Stevie's voice. "I found a cheap place in that trailer court west of Granite Ridge. They didn't even ask for a damage deposit."

Stevie could only imagine the quality of the place. She shuddered and hated that her resolve softened . . . per usual.

"But I don't have a vehicle, of course—and I need to get out now. Today."

Something dark crawled up Stevie's spine. "Why the urgency?"

"He's out for the day, gone to his brother's. If I don't get out now, I don't know when—"

"I'm coming, Mom. I'm coming right now. I have to get my RV ready, but that won't take long. Keep your phone charged and have what you need ready to go. I'll be there in two hours with any luck."

It wasn't until Stevie ended the call that she realized what was different about Marilyn's voice. She'd sounded stressed and scared, but that was nothing entirely new. No, what rang a discordant bell in Stevie's brain was that . . . she sounded sober.

She called Maddie, got voice mail, and left her a quick message saying not to panic if she realized that Stevie had left the resort, explaining—in very brief detail—what she was doing and that she'd be back by evening, hopefully in time to sing a duet with her at Karaoke, ha ha.

Then she texted Jackson. "So sorry, but I have to bail on our plans. Need to help Marilyn. Will come find you when I'm back."

Before she could put her phone down and head outside to start unplugging everything, it rang in her hand. This time it really was Jackson.

"You're going to help *Marilyn*?"

Stevie winced and explained the best she could.

"She doesn't deserve your help."

Stevie shrugged, though, of course, Jackson couldn't see her. "She's my mother, Jackson."

"I get it. Don't move. I'm coming to get you. We'll take my truck. It'll be faster than your rig, and we can load her stuff in the box, maybe even take more things than you'd be able to fit in the motorhome."

"But—"

"No buts. Please let me do this with you. Let me help you help her."

Stevie hesitated, then gave in to what her heart desperately wanted. "Okay."

Jackson must've been ready to walk out the door to meet

her when she'd texted because she'd barely snapped lids on travel dishes with food and water for Syd and got into her coat and boots when he pulled up in front of the RV in his Silverado extended cab.

She was about to lock up, then changed her mind. "One sec," she called. When she re-appeared, she had a big reusable grocery bag full of things from her cupboards and freezer. She handed it to Jackson and zipped around to the passenger side.

"Fancy ride," she said, climbing in and settling Syd's dishes and leash on the cab floor and him on her lap.

"Only the best for my lady," he teased.

"Uh-huh." But their joking fell away quickly as they barrelled away from the lodge, Stevie increasingly grateful for the clear weather. If Marilyn had called during the heavy snow, the roads would've been unpassable. As it was, they were narrow with vast banks of plowed snow on either side, blocking the view. It was like driving in a tunnel.

They drove mostly without talking, Jackson paying attention to the road, but also seeming to intuit that Stevie needed mental space, her brain so full that even small talk might overload it.

They were nearing the exit that would take them to Granite Ridge when Jackson asked, "So do you think whatever has her rattled is real, or she just being a drama queen?"

Marilyn's flat, matter-of-fact tone replayed in Stevie's head. "I think it's real, actually, but considering her high tolerance for terrible guys and even more terrible mistreatment, I don't think I want to know a lot of details." And as it turned out, she wouldn't get to.

Marilyn, with a bag over her shoulder and a pitifully small pile of boxes and one laundry basket of things at her feet, was already waiting in her building's shabby foyer when they got there.

She was pale, older looking, and tinier than Stevie ever

remembered seeing her—almost emaciated. That cut Stevie the deepest. What kind of man victimized someone who was so obviously fragile?

Traces of her prettiness were still there, however, in the bone structure beneath her gaunt cheeks and in the color of her hair—still surprisingly vibrant and unmistakeably Stevie's. Marilyn gave a shy half-smile as they got closer. "Hey, kiddo. Thanks for doing this."

Stevie nodded and introduced Jackson, who took Marilyn's hand and shook it—and didn't say they'd met years earlier.

Briefest of formalities over, Marilyn scanned the street outside the glass doors nervously. "Come on, we should hurry."

Stevie and Jackson did as bidden, and when Jackson loaded the last box, not bothering to use the back of his truck, just stashing everything behind the driver's seat in his extended cab, he asked, "Is that it?"

"It's enough."

"Sure you don't want to grab anything else?"

Marilyn shook her head quickly. "No, it's just stuff. Nothing important."

Stevie shot her a glance. That was one attitude about life that she and Marilyn shared, anyway.

They climbed into the truck, Marilyn taking the passenger side's backseat. When Syd popped his head over Stevie's shoulder to check out the new person, Marilyn made a startled, joyful sound. "Oh, hello, sweetie! Aren't you cute?"

"Would you like to hold him?"

"May I?"

"Of course." Stevie passed him over, and he snuggled into Marilyn's bony lap like he'd known her forever. Marilyn stared down at him, transfixed. Stevie watched them for a second, then turned back to face the front and clicked on her seatbelt.

"So where to?" Jackson asked. Marilyn gave an address, and they started off. There wasn't a lot of conversation. What, after all, did they have to say to each other? It was just one more thing—in a very long list—that made Stevie sad when it came to Marilyn. They shared blood and not much else.

"Are you going to be okay in this new place, you think?"

"Well, it's furnished, so that's one thing. And the landlord promises it doesn't have bedbugs, so that's an excellent start."

Stevie had to close her eyes for a moment. Marilyn settled for . . . so little. "I meant . . . will you be safe or will this Hank guy . . . hassle you?"

Jackson cleared his throat, and Marilyn shifted in her seat and peered out the window as if mentioning Hank's name might conjure him. She laughed nervously. "He's really lazy. I think it'll be out of sight, out of mind."

"Are you going to tell me what's going on? Why the emergency-speed exit?"

Marilyn stared out the window at the blur of gas stations and light industrial shops they passed as they neared the outskirts of Granite Ridge. "No," she finally said. "I've never been much of a mother as you well know, but at least I can spare you that. He's a bad guy is all. A really bad guy."

A fresh upwelling of sorrow threatened to pull Stevie under, but then a strong hand clasped her knee and squeezed gently. Jackson. That's why he'd come: so she wouldn't drown.

"How are you going to live? You on assistance?"

"I've got a job, actually." Marilyn's gaze was still trained on the distant horizon, but her voice had changed. Was a little defiant or edgy or something—as if expecting Stevie's skepticism.

"That's great. Where?"

"At a donut shop. They hired me online, so they haven't laid eyes on me yet. That might be the deal-breaker.'

"Don't be silly, you've got this. You can do it."

Marilyn's gaze jerked from the window and met Stevie's in the rearview mirror. "You think so?"

"Yeah, Mom. I do," Stevie said softly. Something flashed in Stevie's mind then—a happy memory of her and Marilyn. It was such a rare, rare thing she almost shielded her eyes at the painful brightness of it. "Remember how we used to get those homemade jelly-filled donuts from that little place on the corner when we lived on 16th?"

"Omigoodness, yes. Dipped in fine granulated sugar, not powder."

Stevie smiled.

"You remember that too?" Marilyn said though the answer was obvious since Stevie was the one who brought it up.

"Yeah, totally."

They were all quiet again—and while it wasn't an unhappy silence, it was heavy. And then Syd let out a loud, snuffling snore. They all laughed, and the atmosphere lightened.

"You seem too little for such a big noise," Marilyn crooned. Then, speaking toward the window again, as if to herself, she added, "I might get myself a dog. I think that might be a much better plan than a new man."

Jackson squeezed Stevie's knee again. When she glanced at him, his eyes were still trained on the road, but his eyebrows shot up to his hairline. Despite all the complex emotions rolling through her at a high boil, Stevie giggled. Then she caught Marilyn's eye in the rearview mirror again. Marilyn's lips quirked as if even she could see the hilarious obviousness in her comment. Suddenly both she and Stevie were laughing out loud, with genuine shared mirth. It wasn't much of a connection, but it was something.

The buildings grew further apart and farther between, and then there was a storage rental place and big truck stop gas station by a row of shops—a diner, a bargain clothes outlet, and "Ye olde Donut Shoppe."

"Yep, that'd be the one—my new career," Marilyn said drily before Jackson or Stevie asked the question aloud.

And then there was a big sign announcing, "Wilde Wood Trailer Park."

"They really like to throw a classy extra 'e' into words around here," Marilyn said—again voicing a humorous observation that Stevie had also made in her head. "But it's walking distance, that's why I applied."

The trailer—ancient—was surprisingly clean and even had a tiny fenced yard.

"Apparently, there's even a little garden spot somewhere under there," Marilyn said, motioning at the blanket of snow beyond the graying pickets. "I thought I might try my hand at growing something. See if I have a green thumb."

"That'd be so awesome!" Stevie said, unable to keep the hope from her voice.

"I knew you'd approve."

They unloaded Marilyn's stuff in a blink, and she stared goggle-eyed at the big bag of food Stevie handed her. "You shouldn't have. It's too much."

"Just take it. Enjoy it."

Finally, she nodded, but insisted they let her unpack by herself and "hit the road so they could get back while it was still mostly light."

"Is she clean?" Jackson asked when they signaled back onto the highway.

Stevie frowned and stared out the window for a moment, then turned to him. "I don't know. Maybe. I think so—yes, she seems like it."

He raised an eyebrow. "Why didn't you ask?"

She shook her head, tersely. "Because it doesn't matter. If she's not, there's nothing I can do about it. If she is, it won't last . . . but it won't keep me from hoping, and that's just a recipe for disappointment, you know?"

Jackson shot her another look, then shoulder-checked and pulled over on the side of the road.

"What are you doing?"

"You'll see." He lifted the console that sat between them until it clicked into place, creating a bench seat in the front. He patted the space beside him. "Scoot in."

Stevie undid her seatbelt and "scooted." Nestled against Jackson's side, she buckled up again, and he put his arm around her.

"I feel like I'm in a 90s country music video," she said as he commenced driving once more.

"There are worse things, sweetheart," he drawled.

On the way back to the lodge, they stopped to gas up and grabbed burgers and fries to go. The food, though not fancy, really hit the spot. Stevie felt amazingly even-keeled, considering she'd just seen Marilyn. And she knew her peace of mind was all down to Jackson.

She dipped a fry in mayo and held it out. Jackson obligingly chomped it down. "I want to thank you," she said when she was done hand feeding him.

"What for?"

She shrugged, knowing exactly what for, but struggling with how to articulate it. "A lot of women go crazy for little gifts, or they like pretty words or lots of hugging or whatever . . . but what you did today . . . going out of your way to re-arrange your schedule and help me with something I find difficult, without me even asking you to . . . it means a lot."

"You're welcome, but it's not a big deal. Anyone would've done the same in my place."

She shook her head. "No, that's just it. They wouldn't have."

"Well," Jackson said after a second, "I'm a lucky guy that you're so easy to please, but I still want to buy you diamonds, write you poetry, and hug and kiss and something else you all the time."

Stevie laughed. "Well, okay . . . if you insist."

"So, you know all about my mom issues," Stevie said a while later, "and how little they've changed. How are you and your dad these days?"

"Oh, fine—" Jackson stopped talking abruptly. He glanced at Stevie, then back to the road. "Well, 'fine' in that I've mostly come to terms with the fact that we'll likely never be close."

"I'm sorry."

Jackson shrugged. "It is what it is. For a long time, as you probably remember, I thought he hated me . . . I no longer think that. We just have very different personalities—and polar opposite ideas about what family should be." He looked over at Stevie again and smiled. "This is the first Christmas in a long time that I wasn't one bit lonely."

Stevie's throat clogged, and she raised his hand from where it rested on her knee and pressed it to her mouth, kissing his knuckles. "We're a good pair, aren't we?"

"Absolutely," Jackson's voice was full of confident cheer, "and don't you forget it."

It wasn't that late when they got back to the lodge, but Stevie's day had caught up to her emotionally, and when Jackson said he should go see how the pub was faring and asked if she wanted to come with him, she begged off.

"Do you mind terribly if I just call it a night, and we get together tomorrow morning instead? I'll be terrible company."

He cupped her chin gently and stared deeply into her eyes. "You could never be terrible company for me—but of course, you can have downtime if you need it. I'll see you in the morning."

His goodbye kiss was so tender that she almost changed her mind and ran after him. Once he was out of sight, however, she collapsed onto her couch with Syd, completely overwhelmed, and knew she'd made the right decision. And it wasn't Marilyn who had her feeling this way. Or not just Marilyn, anyway. Stevie was used to stewing over her, and as much as she could successfully sadden Stevie, she no longer had the power to completely derail her. No, it was Jackson who unhinged her.

Being with him today solidified something she'd known ever since they reunited, however hard she fought it or tried to pretend it away. She loved Jackson. And it didn't matter if it was too soon or ridiculous or impossible for a long list of reasons. She *loved* him. She had let herself rely on him. Take comfort in him. And it was . . . terrifying. It gave him so much power over her—

The last thoughts made her wince. There was no pleasing her, was there? If he was casual about things, she worried obsessively that she cared more about him than he did her—and that she'd get hurt. If he acted like he seriously saw them having a future, she stressed about botching everything by being neurotic and screwed up—and that she'd get hurt. That's what so many holdouts in her life came down to, wasn't it? The desire to avoid more . . . *hurt*. It didn't matter if it was understandable, considering her background. She hated that chicken side of her nature.

With those fun thoughts running amuck, she texted Maddie to let her know she was back safe and sound—and wasn't surprised to not get an immediate response. She was probably busy with the daughters who weren't wasting their time being insecure.

She watched some Netflix but couldn't concentrate. Why couldn't she trust that Jackson was all that he appeared to be, that he felt the way he said he did, that he—bizarre as it was —saw things worth caring about in her?

Because you know better, whispered the insidious inner voice she recognized all too well. *You know what happens when you hope.*

Drowsy, she pulled a blanket over her lap but wondered if she should go to bed instead. She would happily succumb to sleep to avoid thinking for a while—but Syd had finally had enough of cuddling and sitting around. He leaped off her lap and danced to the door—then skipped back to her, then back to the door again, all the while looking at her meaningfully.

"All right, all right, I get the hint," she grumbled but smiled despite her crappy mood. He was right, after all. A walk would do them both good.

The night was mild and still—not a star in sight, which explained the less severe temperature—and Stevie stayed clear of the pub areas, not wanting to run into anyone. Syd's dog wisdom had been on point. They'd only been walking for about thirty minutes, but she felt a hundred and thirty times saner. She believed Jackson cared for her. His words—but more importantly, his actions, said he did. But she was right about something else, too. She had to get a grip on her own insecurities once and for all, or they would eat away at their relationship, doom it before it even really started. With that decided—though with no idea how to actually accomplish it —she turned around and headed home.

She had just rounded the far side of the lodge that featured an outdoor seating area, complete with a gorgeous river rock fireplace blazing warmly away—when she saw something that made her freeze her tracks. The place was deserted except for one solitary couple, who were kissing passionately in the glowing firelight. Stevie recognized the woman's pretty hair and stylish turquoise coat straight away. It was Maddie—Maddie and some strange guy. Stevie felt about thirteen again, the way her brain framed the observation. But Maddie? With a man? It was . . . unheard of.

"Mom? What are you doing?" Stevie blurted—and wanted to kick herself the second the inane question escaped her. It was obvious what Maddie was doing, and now Stevie had totally interrupted her romantic moment. She longed to disappear as Maddie jerked out of the man's embrace.

First me, Stevie thought, then Jo and Hailey. Now Maddie! It was like their family had been signed up for a reality TV dating show or something without their knowledge—except, they, apparently, weren't cowards like her. They were all bravely taking their chances. She opened her mouth to make a joke to that effect, but, to her horror, no words poured forth. Instead, she teared up—which was embarrassing beyond words. She stumbled over an apology and turned to flee.

"Oh, honey! Wait! I'm sorry. Stevie, wait!" Maddie sounded as horrified as Stevie felt, though really, it was probably just concern.

Mortified, Stevie stuttered that she was fine, but Maddie was having none of it. She turned to her companion and said something quietly that Stevie didn't fully catch.

As Maddie caught up with Stevie, Stevie decided she'd been wrong. She didn't feel thirteen. She felt eight.

"I'm so sorry," Maddie said. "I didn't mean to shock you."

"That's not it," Stevie snuffled. "I just don't get it. How can you do that?"

"Um, I don't know, honey. I didn't know you were there. I wasn't thinking."

"No." Stevie shook her head, let out a small laugh, and rubbed her eyes. "That's not what I meant. I'm not traumatized by you kissing someone—not at all. I just really need to know how you can even consider loving someone again after what happened to you. You know how much it hurts to love someone and lose them. You know how risky it is to give someone your heart and make yourself vulnerable to them. How can you do this?"

"Stevie," Maddie said, taking Stevie's hands. "You don't think I'm scared? You don't think I'm terrified to offer up my heart and have it get broken again?"

"So why do it? Why not protect yourself and stay safe by not letting anyone in?"

"Oh, sweetheart. Loving anyone is a risk, but it's a risk worth taking. What would life be without love? Think of the love you have for your sisters and the love they have for you. That's possible because all of you were willing to make yourselves vulnerable."

"That's different," Stevie said, pulling her hands from Maddie's grasp. "They're my family. I trust them. I know they're there for me and that they won't let me down. It's not the same. "

"Yes, but love is love, babe. Any time you allow yourself to care deeply for another being, you give them the power to hurt you. But you also give them the ability to make your life richer, more meaningful, deeper. It's only in our vulnerability that we allow ourselves to truly experience love. Otherwise, it's like you're standing on one side of a thick stone wall, and they're standing on the other. How much connection can you possibly get that way?"

"But how do you know if someone loves you as much as you love them?"

Maddie sighed and sat on the bench at the edge of the sidewalk.

"I don't have that answer for you. I wish I did. It would make life so much easier." She patted the bench next to her and waited until Stevie had taken a seat. "You can't know. Obviously, you can look at how they treat you, how much of themselves they're willing to share, or how easy it is for them to put your needs first. But even then, there are no guarantees. That's why they say love is a choice. You just have to choose to love them despite the uncertainty."

She put her arm around Stevie, and they rested their heads together, huddled against the cold. "Think of it like this. When you find someone that makes you feel like you can't imagine your life without them, it may be a greater risk to walk away from that and wonder what might have been, than to take a chance on what could be."

"So, do you think you love him? This guy?"

"Robert? I don't know." But Maddie's smile, a different one than Stevie had ever seen on her face before, told Stevie what Maddie might not even know herself yet. She did love this Robert guy. "There's a spark there, for sure," Maddie continued and went onto explain how she was feeling, what her worries were—but she finished with, "I'd rather see what happens next than not to see him at all. Does that make sense?"

"Yeah, I guess."

"I know it sounds crazy, but it actually takes someone very strong to be willing to be vulnerable. You, my dear, are one of the strongest people I've ever met. You'll know if it's real, Stevie. You just have to trust yourself. Trust your instincts. Trust your heart. And be willing to take a risk when you decide they're worth it."

Stevie scrutinized Maddie's face. Was she just being kind and supportive as usual, or did she actually believe all the things she'd just said about her? If the latter, Stevie wished she could have a quarter of the faith in herself that Maddie had in her. "Okay . . . I'll try." She nodded—then felt her heart lift. Maddie had a boyfriend, and it sounded serious! "Sorry I barged in on your date or whatever."

Stevie stood and turned to offer her hand to Maddie. She pulled her mom up to standing and then hugged her.

"I love you, Mom. I want you to be happy. If you think this is the guy for you, then you've got my blessing."

"Thanks, sweetheart. That means a lot to me, and I love you, too. More than you'll ever know."

"All right," Stevie said as she pulled back. "Go find your guy and finish . . . whatever you were doing. I don't wanna know."

"*Good night*, Stevie."

Stevie laughed. "Good night, Mom."

CHAPTER 19

"Want to paint and sip tonight?" a loud robotic voice blurted. Stevie, sitting on her bed, slathering every part of her body that she could reach with lotion, jumped—then remembered. Right. She'd set her phone to read incoming texts aloud while her hands were covered in goop.

Such extreme moisturization measures were a form of pampering she didn't usually indulge in, but since she'd just returned from lounging in Jo's suite's glorious swimming pool-sized bathtub, she figured she might as well go all out. She'd even waxed and shaved, ooh la la!

"Be careful," Jo had teased when she'd gloated. "Jackson's going to think you're high maintenance, after all."

She liked that her family was cool about her being with Jackson, treating it as normal and nice: tease worthy but not a big deal. If they'd made too much of it, it would've stressed her out.

But back to the text. She thought the number the robot attributed the message to was Jackson's—but it wasn't a question she'd expected from him. She wiped her pointer finger dry on the towel she was sitting on and dabbed at her phone, double-checking the message was actually from him, not one of her sisters or Maddie. Then she replied, "Sure, I'm game to try anything at least once."

A shocked emoji flashed, then the message, "Be careful what you promise strange men."

"Okay, weirdo."

"Seriously, this can't be a first for you?"

"What's that supposed to mean?"

Jackson didn't respond to that query, so she sent another. "Should I meet you somewhere?"

"Nope. I'm on my way to you!"

When he arrived at her door half an hour later, he was laden down with bags. One was filled with bottles, one with what appeared to be groceries, and one had a beautiful cedar board sticking out the top of it.

"I'm confused," she said, gesturing at his full arms.

"Me too. What's with the coat?"

She had started stuffing her arms into her coat when she'd heard him approach; she stopped mid zip and cocked her head. "Aren't we going to a paint and sip night?"

He looked horrified. "Like where we paint a picture and sip things with other people as witnesses?"

"Well . . . yeah. That's what your text said."

"What? Really? No! I asked, or meant to ask, if you wanted to do a wine and cheese night. Auto-fill must've gone crazy or something."

Stevie started laughing. "Okay, that does make more sense."

"And you're still in?"

"Definitely yes, with even more enthusiasm, actually." She winked. "But I have to confess, you're right. Not my first time."

"But it will be your best time."

"Promises, promises."

He set the bags down and pulled her into a rowdy kiss. "And a threat."

As he started pulling out food and arranging it on the board, Stevie took in the offerings and glanced down at the leggings and shirt she'd donned for a painting date.

"No looking!" she squealed.

Of course, he looked.

"No, seriously, give me five minutes. No peeking."

"But now I really, really want to peek," he complained, but obligingly closed his eyes.

"Ta-dah," Stevie said a moment later.

"Wow," Jackson gave her—and the little black dress she was wearing—an appreciative ogle. "I mean I do have a sweatshirt fetish, but this . . . this is nice too."

A few minutes later, while she lit candles, Jackson paused in the last steps of plating and watched her.

"What?" she finally asked.

"You just really are so beautiful. In everything you wear."

She felt her cheeks warm. "Maybe it's dumb, but you actually do . . . make me feel pretty."

Jackson smiled. "Well, 'pretty' is a start anyway—and I do really, really like that dress."

"Oh yeah?"

"Yeah, it gives me all this access to your gorgeous neck."

In addition to an indecently decadent variety of cheeses, including a sensual smoked gouda, a gorgeous Camembert, and a sharp horseradish infused cheddar that Stevie was particularly enamored with, Jackson had brought booze to go with each offering. A young Pinot Noir for the gouda, dry apple cider for the Camembert, Riesling for the cheddar, plus a plethora of reds for everything else.

Stevie, mindful of genetics, wasn't a huge drinker but

even going slow and aiming for more cheese than booze, it wasn't long before she was totally . . . glowing.

Syd, not wanting to be left out of the fun, kept begging, and Stevie kept apologizing to him. "Sorry, Syd. Cheese is not for dogs." The line was hilarious to both Stevie and Jackson— funnier to them than it would've been to anyone else—and they each randomly repeated it throughout the night, even when Syd had long given up on getting any.

Jackson was on Syd's side, but followed Stevie's lead and didn't give him cheese. "Have you ever noticed people are much stricter about their dogs' diets than about their own?"

Stevie laughed. "I've never really thought about it before, but yes, come to think of it, Ed—and now Syd—definitely seem to feel there's an unfair double standard."

At some point, though, Stevie reached her limit. She pushed back from the table, hands on her stomach. "Ugggh, sooo good, but sooo full. I am . . . *done*."

"Finally. I've been trying to match you bite for bite, but I thought you were going to eat me under the table."

"Ha ha, I think you held your own."

"Seriously, though, I don't know what hit me harder, the cheese or the booze."

Stevie giggled and smacked his arm.

"What was that for?" Jackson looked amused.

"I wanted to be in the who-hits-harder competition."

"You're wasted!"

"No, I'm not *wasted*." Stevie laughed uproariously before she even got to her punchline. "I'm *super* wasted."

"*Wow*." Jackson grinned appreciatively.

Their jokes didn't get any better from there, but they continued to find themselves beyond hilarious—and laughed until they almost cried when Syd side-eyed them and shook his head like he disapproved. They both also agreed it was good there were no witnesses. They knew how funny they were—and that no one who hadn't been hitting the cheese all night would understand.

Later, another cheese joke (that you had to be there for to find remotely funny) led to a massage. As Stevie reclined, feet in Jackson's lap, her head lolling back with pleasure, she groaned dramatically, "Ohhh, that's soooo good. What am I going to do without you? I can't bear the thought!"

Jackson stopped rubbing and clasp her foot instead. "Marry me."

Stevie burst out laughing. "But our engagement story will be so . . . cheesy."

Syd looked at her, sighed, then hopped down off the arm of the couch and went to bed—his first time willingly claiming Ed's old terrain. Stevie giggled so hard she started to hiccup. "I don't think he appreciates my wit."

Jackson was smiling. "I do, as you know—and I'm serious."

"We can't be married." She motioned wildly around the RV. "There's no one to officiate."

"I bet there's an app."

"No way. You can't get married online. That's not a thing . . . is it?"

Jackson was already on his phone, and she was peering over his shoulder. A few minutes later, they both cheered. "I knew it!" he said.

"Well, how can we not?" she replied.

"And that is how Miss Stevie Fox ended up married to Jackson Elmsworth

Bassett via the Internet," Jackson intoned in his quickly becoming famous—to Stevie only—snooty accent a few minutes later.

"Elmsworth! I'd forgotten your middle name. I would've married you for that."

"Shh, I need to do something."

"What?"

"Kiss my bride."

Jackson's mouth, velvet soft and warm, found hers. Stevie felt the buzz of alcohol wane from her system, as a much sweeter, all-encompassing intoxication took over.

CHAPTER 20

P ale wintery sunshine streamed around the edges of the blinds, and the RV was bright with light when Stevie woke up on the verge of laughter at some detail that was already sliding away from her. She'd had the funniest dream about Jackson . . .

She rolled to her side and saw him spread out beside her, limbos akimbo, his skin radiating heat, though nothing covered him but a sheet. Unable to resist touching him, she gently rubbed the sexy stubble line on his jaw, then pressed her lips to his temple and breathed in deeply. Just the scent of him—

Still out for the count, he smiled and nuzzled at her hand for a moment but didn't stir other than that.

"You sleep like the dead," she whispered fondly and enjoyed the luxury of being able to watch him for as long as she wanted—would it ever be enough?—without him knowing about it.

The dreamy past week and bits and snippets of last night played through her head, and she bit her lip to keep from laughing out loud in sheer . . . surprise, glee, delight, *love*.

Outside a cloud must've scudded across the sun. The RV,

so bright and cheerful, was suddenly a gloomy gray—and just like that, staring down at her . . . *husband*, Stevie felt . . . sick.

She wanted to blame it on being hungover but knew it was worse than that. It was how much she wanted this—to be married to Jackson for real, for him to be her husband, for better or worse, not just as a wine-fueled joke. She'd been well aware of the problematic intensity of her feelings for Jackson—but she'd honestly had no clue about the full depths of her fantasies surrounding him. And she couldn't tell him she wanted the marriage to be real. He would think she was crazy—and not in a good way, in a desperate-for-love-Marilyn-way—and she would lose him for good. It was waaaaay too soon.

It was a good thing she knew the RV as well as she knew her own body. She slid around Jackson, climbed out of bed, and got dressed all without making a sound. Syd must've sensed something was up because he waited for her by the door, excitedly wagging his stub of a tail—but was quiet about it.

She couldn't be here when Jackson woke up and had a good laugh at their silly, non-legally binding joke. Her hurt would show. She needed to go for a walk and get a grip on herself so that she could smile and joke too. Hopefully, then they could keep seeing each other, him none the wiser about the level of her pathetic insanity.

Grabbing a leash and her coat, Syd on her heels, she silently exited the motorhome and latched the door behind her. The frigid air nipped hard at her still bed-warm body, and she longed—in all ways, for all reasons—to turn back. But she didn't. She couldn't. Shivering, she did up her coat and grabbed her gloves from her pocket.

It didn't escape her notice—and yes, it was heartbreakingly unfair—that like a dumbass, she'd opened herself up to someone, and now she was the one leaving her home. Again.

She hadn't gotten very far when she heard Jackson calling her name. Well, truthfully, Syd heard first—and stopped and pulled in Jackson's direction. Pretending she didn't hear him wouldn't work with Syd prancing and skipping in excitement to see him, so, despite the fact she had no better control over her emotions than she had minutes ago when she left, she pasted on a cheery smile and turned around.

"Hey, sleepyhead. What's up?"

"*Stevie,*" Jackson repeated, still a couple feet away, sounding urgent and tortured. Stevie was instantly on high alert. Good grief, she'd thought him teasing and joking about their Internet marriage would be awful. If he was going to put her through a serious, heartfelt explanation of how last night was just a joke, like she seriously needed the heads up, she was going to die of humiliation.

Do not cry, you ninny, she commanded herself. Do not.

"I thought you left."

"Um, I did. . . . to take Syd for a pee?"

"You weren't freaking out?"

She bit her lip. What did he want from her?

He was close enough to touch her now, and he did, taking her gently by both arms, staring into her face as if searching for something. Then he shook his head. "Okay, I admit it. I'm the one freaking out."

"About?"

He shook his head again. "You're going to think I'm a total loser, but . . . I need to tell you how I really feel."

Here it comes, Stevie thought sadly.

"Please don't think less of me or worry that I'm bodies-in-the-basement nuts."

Stevie had to smile at that. "You know if you're trying to convince someone you're not dangerously crazy, that probably shouldn't be your go-to example."

"Right, right." Jackson nodded like she was giving him sincere and sage advice.

She took pity on him, feeling better. She wanted him in her life in whatever capacity he was up for. If that made her pathetic and needy . . . and vulnerable, well, sucked to be her. "Don't worry. I'm not expecting my ring any second now. We were drunk and—"

"No, that's just it. We were drunk, so we—or I—did what I really wanted to do, inhibitions be damned. Got married."

Stevie stared at him.

"I know our Internet wedding wasn't legally binding, and on some level I know we were both just having a gag—of course, I know that—but when I woke up this morning, I rolled over to say 'Good morning, wife!' and you weren't there . . ."

Stevie bit her lip. Syd danced. Jackson went on. "Suddenly, I realized, as lame as you'll probably think I am, that's exactly what I want. You as my wife. For real. I want to . . . treat it like it was real."

Stevie could only bite her lip harder and stare some more. Syd actually stopped dancing, as if he was in painful suspense now too.

"I get that you might not feel the same, and I'm happy to keep dating for as long as you need, but to respect myself, I have to put it all on the table. It wasn't, it *isn't*, a joke, for me. I loved you all through senior year and meeting you again now, as an available adult . . . it's like coming home."

More staring. And an uncomfortable feeling in Stevie's chest—like her heart was beating so hard it might literally explode.

Jackson shifted foot-to-foot. He was still holding her arms, and now he rubbed his hands up and down them briskly, like she was cold and he was trying to warm her. She realized in his haste to come find her, he'd forgotten to put on a jacket. Something hot and bright kindled inside her.

"And if you're worried about living arrangements. Don't.

If living in a motorhome for all of our days is what you need to feel safe and in control, I'm in."

He hung his head then as if her silence had gotten to him, and he was sure she was going to reject him. . . .

She removed a glove and put her palm to his cold face. "Funny, I was trying to get my courage up to tell you the same thing, that if you'd give us a try, if you'd love me, I'd be happy in a house, in a condo, in a whatever, wherever you are, but I was sure you would think I was desperate or unbalanced or something, and that I'd lose you for good."

"Really?"

Stevie nodded, widening her eyes to show how much she meant it. Then she made one amendment. "Well, live anywhere with you as long it comes equipped with a gas stove."

Jackson cocked an eyebrow and gave her a mock incredulous look. "Well, of course, wife. That goes without saying. We're crazy, but we're not insane."

They locked eyes, and something seismic shifted within Stevie. Was she still afraid of being hurt? No—she was terrified of it. Did she now deeply understand how worthy of love and decent treatment she was? No—but she'd keep working on that. Did she believe some things were worth the risk of getting hurt or being humiliated or abandoned? Yes—absolutely. Some people would think they were jumping in too fast or making a mistake. But for her, the real mistake would be failing to take a leap of faith and refusing to believe in love when she'd been so fortunate and had experienced so much of it. . . .

CHAPTER 21

Stevie did her best to wear a poker face as she walked into the lodge's New Year's Eve party on Jackson's tuxedoed arm, but the way random strangers kept beaming at her, she was obviously failing and revealing just how happy she was. And the joyful feeling of being in a dream that she never wanted to awaken from lasted throughout the evening. From the smiles on her sisters' faces —and Maddie's—the odd time or two that they whirled past each other on the dance floor, she could see they were experiencing similar feelings.

They paused to grab refreshments at the bountiful buffet table while the band was on a break. Jackson kept one arm around her, even while he snacked. Together they took in the high ceiling, strung with a million tiny white lights, and the three massive crystal balls that sent rainbows of color bouncing throughout the room.

"It's so beautiful," she whispered.

"You are," he agreed. She crossed her eyes. He grinned, and as the jazz band started a new set, he guided her back to the dance floor and pulled her into a soft, swaying waltz. Stevie wanted the night to go on and on and on.

When her family members caught up with each other for a midnight toast, something they'd arranged to do earlier in the day, her sisters gave her big smiles but also looked . . . curious.

"Look at you!" Jo said, reaching to touch Stevie's soft flowy white evening dress.

"You're as pretty as a bride."

Jackson looked down at her and winked. Unfortunately, Jo, never one to miss anything, caught the look. She cocked her head and scrutinized Stevie, who widened her eyes and tried not to look so *obviously* like a person *obviously* trying to keep a secret.

"It's gorgeous," Alissa agreed. "I'm glad you didn't wear this at my wedding. You would've totally outshone me."

"Not a chance," Stevie said at the same time as Jed said, "No way." Stevie grinned. Jed really was okay.

"Does this mean you're not going to wrangle your way into helping in a kitchen tonight?" Hailey teased.

"No promises," Stevie said. Everyone laughed.

"You look so happy, honey," Maddie said softly.

"I am . . . and I'd like you to meet someone important." Stevie pulled Jackson forward.

In perfect sync, like it was a comedy skit or something, each of her family members tilted their heads and gave her an odd look.

Maddie's brow furrowed. "We've all met Jackson, dear. We knew him when you two were such good . . . friends as teenagers. And we met him again, of course, when he saved our rehearsal dinner." She turned toward him. "I can't thank you enough, Jackson. Stevie was right to rave about you. You're a fantastic cook."

Jackson dipped his head and purred in Stevie's ear, too quiet for anyone else to hear. "You *raved* about me? Do tell."

Stevie grinned. "Shut up."

Maddie looked shocked.

"Sorry, Mom. Not you. *Him*." She tugged Jackson's sexy jacket lapel, pulling him to her side. "I know you've met Jackson, but have I introduced you to my husband?"

"Your . . . " Maddie looked at her, and Stevie was choked up by the expression she saw in her mom's eyes. She recognized it. It was the same love, pride—and maternal concern—Stevie saw in Maddie's face whenever she looked at any of her sisters.

"Yes," Stevie affirmed.

"Well, that explains our heart-to-heart the other night." Maddie patted Stevie's arm, then turned to Jackson. "Welcome to the family."

Continuing the unnecessary introductions in a joking voice, Stevie made a flourishing gesture. "And Jackson, this is—"

Jackson finished for her. "Your lovely soul mother."

Stevie sucked in a breath. She'd told Jackson she, Jo, Hailey, and Alissa referred to each other as soul sisters, initially because Maddie had encouraged them to see each other that way when they first met, but then, as they grew up together, because it was the only fitting description for their close relationship. Their bond, forged by similar losses and the *choice* to be family, was at least as strong as any blood tie could ever be.

She'd never thought of Maddie in that exact term. However, it was, of course, precisely what she was. And it clarified some of her confusion and guilt surrounding Marilyn too. Marilyn was her biological mother, and she couldn't stop loving her, though their relationship was complex and difficult, and might always be, no matter how Stevie wished differently. But Maddie? Maddie was the mother of her heart. Her soul mother. It was perfect. Jackson's fingers laced through hers and squeezed gently like he was reading her thoughts.

"This probably seems like it's coming out of the blue, Mrs.
—"

"Mom," Maddie stressed.

"Mom," Jackson agreed, smiling shyly, and though they
hadn't talked about it explicitly since they were teenagers,
Stevie knew how much Jackson had always longed for a
mother. Maddie's kindness would be as special for him as it was
for Stevie herself. "I never got over Fox here, so when I got the
chance to lock her down and trick her into saying 'I do' before
her overactive fight or flee instincts kicked in, I had to take it."

"He knows you well," Jo said approvingly.

"It's so cute that he still calls you Fox!" Hailey added.
Stevie rolled her eyes.

"If you guys got yourselves organized a few days earlier,
we could've had a double wedding," Alissa chimed in.

"Oh yeah, Jed would've loved that," Stevie said.

Jed winked. "As long as you passed through a metal
detector and no alarm went off, I'd have been good with it."

"Anyway," Jackson continued, "I look forward to getting
to know you all again, and I promise, though our vows were
made quickly, they weren't done lightly. I will love Stevie the
best that I can every day for the rest of our lives." He stuck
out his hand to shake Maddie's in a formal greeting, but she
spread her arms and welcomed him into a hug.

"I also need to thank you. Stevie says if it wasn't for you,
she wouldn't know how to cook—oh, and that you literally
saved her life."

"I see you both prioritize cooking over everything else.
That's a relief."

Stevie laughed.

There was a jumble of chat and much laughter for another
few minutes. Then a host appeared with a tray of champagne.
Maddie looked at her watch. "Perfect timing. Quick, everyone! Grab your champagne!"

They each took a flute, and a few minutes later, it was time.

"Ten . . . nine . . . eight . . .," they chanted in perfect unison. "Seven . . . six . . . five . . . four . . . three. . . two . . . " Jackson squeezed Stevie's hand, and she squeezed back. "One!" they all cheered in unison. "Happy New Year!"

They toasted one another, and hugs and kisses were exchanged all around.

"Okay," Maddie said when everyone had taken a sip. "What's on everyone's mind? Make a wish, set a goal, or make a toast."

One by one, they did just that. When it was Stevie's turn, she looked up into Jackson's beloved face. It was impossible to believe that not even two weeks ago, she had been feeling unfulfilled and blue . . . and now dreams she hadn't even fully admitted to herself were coming true. They'd file official paperwork early in the new year, so their marriage was recognized by the powers that be, not just themselves, and they'd have some sort of big party. From the way her sisters and Maddie were glowing—and from the surprising toasts and wishes so far, there'd be lots to celebrate.

Taking in their precious faces, Stevie had only one thing to say.

"I . . . don't have a toast or a wish or a goal this year," she confessed. Her family looked concerned. She swallowed a huge lump forming in her throat as she remembered their first Christmas together and all their years since. "I just have a huge thank you. Thank you for being the family I always longed for when I was young. Thank you for your patience and for seeing good in me that I don't always see myself. You guys mean the world to me—and you'll never believe it, but I'm so excited about all our changes. Just . . . *thank you.* "

There was a soft silence, then Maddie said, "Aw, sweetie . . . you're so welcome."

Everybody cheered and sipped, and then it was the next person's turn to toast.

Stevie's hand was warm in Jackson's, and for quite possibly the very first time in her life, Stevie didn't need to dream. She was perfectly happy in the moment, exactly the way it was unfolding.

EPILOGUE

At Jackson's prompting, their staff deserted their training session and flooded outside sans jackets, eager for the big reveal. Now, stamping their feet lightly and blowing into their clenched fists for warmth in the blustery afternoon chill, they gathered beneath the veiled sign in the small courtyard, buzzing with excitement.

No one was more eager to discover the secret name Jackson had come up with for their family-style pub than Stevie was, though. Part of her was still blown away that she'd let him have all the fun of naming it without her—and another part was even more blown away at how totally secure he'd kept the secret.

"Drumroll, please!" Jackson hollered, reveling in every second of the drama. A couple of servers obliged, rapping out a rhythm on the side of the brick building.

Jackson whipped the canvas sheet free of the sign in one fluid movement and bowed theatrically.

Loud applause, whistling catcalls, and rowdy cheers filled the air, but Stevie didn't make a sound. She was on the verge of tears. How on earth hadn't she guessed? It was beyond perfect. It was amazing.

Curled up together on a plaid cushion, a floppy-eared dog and a sleek red fox graced an old-fashioned enamel sign that swung gently on a wrought iron hanging bracket. "Fox & Hound," it announced in large gold letters.

"Oh, Jackson," she breathed when he jumped down from his perch on the sign's stone mount and came over to her. "It's . . . I . . ."

His smile said he knew exactly what it was that she was struggling to articulate, and he wrapped his arm around her shoulder and studied the sign from her perspective. "Happy almost anniversary, Fox," he whispered.

Anniversary. How could they have already been married for almost a year? It seemed impossible like they'd tied the knot just days ago. And yet . . . here they were, set up in Granite Ridge, about to open their dream venture with a reliable staff and another excellent chef, so they could have their pub and regular days off too—something Jackson insisted on. She turned and pulled her husband into a kiss, trying to convey everything she felt for him in that age-old way. Some of their staff clapped, and she waved her hand to shoo them off.

"Are you glad I kept it a secret? Did it make it more special?" he asked a few minutes later.

"Secret or common knowledge from the time you thought of it, I don't think anything could've made it more special," she replied honestly. "And as for the secret, fair's fair. I have a surprise for you too. Although it's not quite accurate to imply that I've been working on it all by myself."

Jackson smiled, but his head tilted. "I feel there's a riddle in there . . . but I don't get it."

"Sucks to be you then, I guess." Stevie grinned, then took one of his hands and placed it on her still-flat stomach. His brow creased, and one eyebrow shot up.

"I was going to keep quiet until we open on Christmas Eve, but—"

Stevie saw Jackson figure out what she was saying as clearly as if a lightbulb flashed over his head.

"Are we . . . are you?"

She nodded. "Yep. Fox, Hound, and Baby."

This time—this rare time—it was Jackson who was speechless. He held her out at arm's length and studied her, then, laughing out loud, he pulled her close and kissed her, and kissed her, and kissed her.

"Do you know how lucky we are?" he asked, his voice full of wonder.

Stevie just nodded. She did know. Marilyn was still, knock on wood, working and apparently doing okay. She had adopted a sweet, middle-aged Newfie who weighed more than she did. It made Stevie smile every time she thought about it. Her father-in-law was, to both her and Jackson's surprise, pleased by their marriage and tried to make a monthly meal together a priority. She had her soul sisters and her soul mother—and now she had her soul mate and would soon have a little family all her own. Yes, she was . . . beyond lucky. Her blessings had surpassed all of her dreams.

She knew Maddie and her sisters felt the same. After their first Christmas together, when they'd become a family all those years ago, none of them would've guessed another Christmas could ever mean as much. Yet their Christmas at Cedar Mountain Lodge may have been even more life-changing. So much had happened to and for them all! Even Alissa, whose Christmas Rings—Stevie cut off that thought. Though she never tired of the story—and had apparently gotten it all wrong, she found out later—Alissa's story wasn't hers to tell. Anyone who, like her, couldn't get enough of the Soul Sisters at Cedar Mountain Lodge could read all about it themselves.

Don't miss a book in SOUL SISTERS AT CEDAR MOUN-
TAIN LODGE and read on for a sneak peek of the next story
in the series, *Christmas Rings*.

Book 1: Christmas Sisters – prologue book

Book 2: Christmas Kisses by Judith Keim

Book 3: Christmas Wishes by Tammy L. Grace

Book 4: Christmas Hope by Violet Howe

Book 5: Christmas Dreams by Ev Bishop

Book 6: Christmas Rings by Tess Thompson

And some more fun: join the authors in the Soul Sisters
Book Chat Facebook Group for book discussions, activities,
and interaction with other book lovers!

Alissa yawned as she slipped out of her jeans and sweater and into her skimpy cocktail waitress uniform of booty shorts and a bikini top. Friday nights tried her willpower and resolve. After a long week of teaching kindergarten, coming to the gentlemen's club to place drinks in front of men who should have been home with their wives or families was not exactly her dream life. However, sometimes even a nice girl had to do what she had to do. Even if it meant keeping aspects of her life a secret from her mother and sisters. This made her cringe when she thought about the perpetual lie. They were not a family of secrets. Maddie had always told them they could tell her whatever was on their mind, even if it wasn't pretty.

But this? This job she wouldn't understand. Alissa wouldn't have done it had she not been desperate. After graduation, she took a hard look at her student loans and wondered how she would ever pay them off with only her kindergarten teacher salary. Maddie would insist that she help Alissa financially. With everything in her being, Alissa didn't want that to happen. Maddie Kirby had already sacrificed enough. Using her savings was not the answer to Alissa's debt. She would take care of this herself. One way or the other.

She'd swallowed her pride and accepted the job, burying her shame about lying to her family. For a year, she slogged through shifts, narrowly escaped gropes, and put every tip she made into the bank.

Having accomplished her goals, she'd been down to her last month of waitressing. College loans were paid. She'd even managed to buy a few pieces of furniture for her tiny apartment. There was even a little extra in the bank for the unexpected. But then, her best friend Sophie had been in a car accident. She'd almost been killed. Multiple fractures to her legs, broken ribs and a concussion made it impossible for her to work.

When Alissa got the call about Sophie, her heart stopped. Memories of her parents' deaths and the toll they had taken on her life rushed over her. Only when the nurse assured her that Sophie would live could she breathe. However, Sophie wouldn't be able to return to her office assistant job for months. An hourly employee without adequate insurance and no income, she would accumulate debt faster than she could heal. Alissa couldn't let that happen. They'd been best friends since they were little kids. Even after Alissa had had to change schools, the girls had remained close. Sophie had been the only person from her old life that she hadn't lost. She would do anything for her, including staying on at the club for a few more months.

The gentlemen's club was on the higher end, if that was possible for such a place. It was clean. A bright red and blue rug gave the room a cheery feel despite the dim lights. The stage was simple and elevated from the patrons' tables to make it less likely for a lusty grab. Their dancers didn't strip down all the way, just to their bras and panties. Okay, yes, the bras were basically see-through, but it was the principle of the thing. That's what she told herself anyway. Also, there was absolutely no touching allowed. Even lap dances. Alissa never could figure out how they managed to keep their distance, dancing so close without actually touching. No matter what anyone said, there were skills involved in the profession. That's why she was only a waitress. She couldn't dance to save her life.

The patrons were nicely dressed, usually rich businessmen entertaining clients. Alissa would rather have had a nice steak if it were her being wined and dined. But who was she to judge? They tipped well, not just the dancers but Alissa too. Rarely, a table would get out of hand. When that happened, Rif, the owner, kicked them out as soon as he caught even a hint of trouble. He took care of his girls, he always said. The girls, in turn for his loyalty and fairness, were loyal right back.

Alissa had been surprised to learn more about the girls as time went on. They were not what she'd expected. There were a few law school and graduate students, single mothers without child support, even a medical student. They could make more money dancing than they could ever hope to make elsewhere. Alissa came to admire them, these women who put their real lives aside every night to entertain men because they had to.

Alissa simply delivered cocktails. No dancing for her, she'd told Rif up front. He'd told her the opportunity was available if she ever changed her mind. "You could make ten times what you're making slinging drinks and you sure have the body for it."

"No, thank you, sir," she'd said. It was bad enough that she had to wear scarcely more than a bikini. There was no way she was prancing around a pole or giving men lap dances.

This particular Friday night was busy. She scampered from table to table, delivering drinks and taking orders. Music blasted through the speakers as the girls came out, one by one, to perform. They each had a persona that matched the song. Millie, for example, the medical student, danced to a country song while dressed in a tight "farmer's daughter" outfit, including a straw hat and two blond braids.

The song was nearing the end when Alissa stopped at a table of four men in suits. They'd just arrived and were in the process of taking off their jackets and loosening ties when she asked what she could get them. She guessed two of them to be in their early thirties. Both wore wedding rings and were attractive in that generic, closely cropped, business guy type of way. The third, who seemed a few years younger than the others, had dark, floppy hair and intelligent, sensitive eyes the color of unwashed denim. She felt certain she'd seen him before but couldn't place where. The fourth man was closer to sixty, given his mostly gray hair and creases on his forehead and around his eyes. He winked at her when she turned toward him. She blatantly ignored the flirtatious overture and asked him, flatly, what he wanted.

"We'd like martinis," Denim Eyes said. "Made from Marsh Vodka, please."

Her eyebrows lifted before she could stop them. That was the highest-end vodka they sold, made by the boutique Marsh distillery. Rif said they made the finest liquors in the world. Alissa wouldn't know. She occasionally had a glass of wine after her shift, but liquor made her gag.

"Only the best for this table," the old man said. "Since Marsh here has the tab." He pointed at Denim Eyes.

Marsh? Was he the owner of the distillery? "Stirred or shaken?" Alissa asked at the same time Millie pranced over to the side of the stage directly in front of Marsh's table and shook everything. Great timing, Alissa thought. She must not have been the only one who noticed the symmetry of word and action. Everyone but Marsh tittered as Millie lifted a red cowgirl-boot-clad leg and shimmied around a pole.

"Shaken, please." Denim Eyes' cheeks had turned bright

red. Or, Mr. Marsh, she thought. He shifted in his chair and scratched behind his ear as he looked away from the stage.

"Olives or twists?" Alissa asked.

"I like them dirty, as dirty as they come," Gray Hair said before whipping his head back to the stage where Gayle was making her entrance in a naughty nurse outfit to the tune of "Hurts So Good."

"Twist for me, please," Marsh said, not meeting Alissa's gaze.

The other two asked for olives, without the sexual innuendo.

Alissa scurried off to the bar. Rif tended bar on Friday nights, along with Marty, a crusty former sailor who Alissa adored.

"Four Marsh martinis, up. One with a twist, the other three with olives. One dirty."

"You got it, little lady," Marty said. He was the type who could call a woman *little lady* and get away with it—at least with her. He was from a different time, so Alissa cut him some slack. Her sisters Stevie and Jo would not have. They had no patience for that kind of thing.

Rif set a pitcher of beer on the counter.

"See that table?" she said, indicating with a slight nudge toward Marsh and his friends. "Do you know him? The young, cute one?"

"Sure. That's Jed Marsh. Of Marsh Vodka," Rif said. "He comes in during the day usually—just to do business. I've never seen him here at night."

"I got the feeling he's entertaining clients," Alissa said. "And that he's not thrilled to be here."

"He's a straight-and-narrow type of guy," Rif said. "His old man runs the show but supposedly the business will be passed down to him in the next few years."

While the guys fixed the drinks, she took the pitcher of beer to a table of men who looked like they belonged in a fraternity house. By the time she returned, Rif had four martinis on a platter for her.

"Marsh hasn't taken his eyes off you," Rif said.

"Me?"

"Yeah, you. Be careful," Rif said. "His mother's the dragon lady. Runs off every woman he's ever met."

"How do you know?" Alissa asked.

"He's been selling me vodka for a long time," Rif said. "We talk, you know, how men do. I complain about my wife. He complains about his mother. Good man, that one, but his old man's a real piece of work. Throw the mother in there and no wonder he's single."

"I'll keep that in mind," she said. "Not that I'm available or anything."

"You're not?" Rif asked.

"Who dates a girl that works in a place like this?" Alissa asked.

Rif clutched the front of his shirt. "I'm hurt."

"You know what I mean," she said. "Look at this outfit. Am I the type you take home to mama?"

"You're a kindergarten teacher," Marty said.

"By day," Alissa said. "But at night I'm a cocktail waitress in a questionable club." She grinned to let them know she was teasing. Kind of, anyway.

"Off with you," Rif said. "I've had enough of your sassy mouth."

Here's what Alissa had learned during her tenure at the club. People, like Rif and Marty—good people—were in all walks of life. One didn't have to be a pastor to be a good person. In fact, one's profession had nothing to do with the compassion of one's heart. Maddie had always taught them to be openminded, to remember that it was not a human's right to judge another. That right was reserved for God. This lesson had been hammered into Alissa's consciousness since the first night she put on her waitress uniform and met some of the other girls. Before this experience, she might have judged them for their choice of work. Not now. She liked this about herself, that she could see below the surface of a thing and understand that life was complicated. One's journey was not always the straight path one wished it to be. There were boulders that crushed, mountains to climb, rivers to cross.

We were survivors, she'd often thought over the years. The experiences of her sisters and Maddie were proof. What she and her sisters had survived, prior to Maddie making them a family, had changed them, marked them forever. Yet, all the good and bad mingled together to form the complex, phenomenal women they all were.

Even me, she thought, as she dabbed a wet spot on the side of one of the martini glasses. She might not be as smart or ambitious as her sisters, but she had a calling. Those little ones in her class, especially the ones from families struggling financially, inspired her to bring her all every single day. The foundation she gave them would take them through their whole lives. Someday, she would look back and know she'd impacted the world in her small way.

She lifted the tray of martinis, thanking Rif, and headed back to Marsh and his companions. At the table, she placed the extra dirty one next to the dirty old man, careful not to get close enough that his hand could grab her bottom. She set the other two martinis in front of the generic suit guys, then gave the last one to Marsh.

"That's a balancing act," Marsh said, gesticulating toward her tray. "My family appreciates your care. We think every drop of our vodka is precious." He said this with a self-deprecating smile that matched his vocal tone. She liked him, this handsome Marsh, with his kind eyes and good manners. There was a quality about him, perhaps the precise way he moved and his squared shoulders, that reminded her of another era. A time when men kept their eyes focused on a woman's face instead of her chest.

The others at the table? Not so much. At times like this, she wanted to grab the nearest jacket and slip it over her shoulders.

No whining, she told herself. This was the only way to help Sophie.

She smiled sweetly and asked if they'd like anything else.

"We're good for now," Marsh said. "Thank you."

They exchanged a quick smile before she scooted off to the next table. The rest of the night passed quickly. Jed Marsh and his friends stayed for another round of drinks before leaving around midnight. As expected, Marsh paid the bill. She smiled to see the thirty percent tip he left her.

After closing time, she counted her tips at the bar, while Rif and Marty cleaned and put away glasses and mugs. It had been a good night. The dancers were always wound up by the end of the night, so those who didn't have to be home right away were enjoying a cocktail at one of the empty tables. She would have expected them to be too tired to talk, but they chatted away about this and that. Alissa was too tired to even listen but enjoyed the familiar cadence of their voices and their laughter.

"Jed Marsh asked about you," Rif said.

"He did?" She cringed at the high-pitched schoolgirl tone of her words.

"I told him you were single," Rif said. "But that you're one of a kind and perfect, so if he's interested, he has to prove his worthiness first."

"Rif, you didn't?"

"If he's worth his salt, then he'll rise to the challenge," Rif said, shrugging.

"Who exactly does he have to prove his worth to?" Alissa smiled, knowing the answer.

"Me, for one," Rif said. "I can't have him waltzing in here and thinking he can take you out just because he's rich."

"Me, for two," Marty said.

"And what does this dog and pony show look like?" Her grandmother, Nan, used that phrase, and it always made Alissa laugh, imagining a dog and a pony dancing a jig.

"I told him what's necessary," Rif said. "The first step is flowers, with a request for a dinner date. I made sure he understood you would not be picked up so that he could murder you in his car."

"Rif, I don't think he's a murderer," Alissa said, laughing.

"Until we know for sure, you will meet him at the restaurant."

"He hasn't even asked me out yet."

"If he does as asked, there will be flowers and a card delivered here tomorrow," Rif said. "We'll wait and see."

"You two probably scared him away."

"So, you would go out with him?" Marty asked.

"I mean, I guess so. He's cute and has exceptional manners. Other than the goon he was with, he seemed nice."

"We'll see about that," Rif said.

Alissa gathered her bills and blew both men a kiss. "I'll see you tomorrow evening." They really were the dearest, sweetest guys around, even though they were ridiculously overprotective of her and the dancers. She could remember her father being that way too, joking that she wouldn't be allowed to date until she was thirty.

In the dressing room, she peeled her uniform from her tired body and pulled on her jeans and sweatshirt. Rif had a rule that they were not to walk to their cars alone. Millie was ready to go, thankfully.

"Let's do it, girl," Millie said. "I could sleep for a week."

"Me too," Alissa said. She clocked out, calling good-night to the girls who were removing makeup at the bank of mirrors in the dressing room. They all gave friendly waves before Alissa and Millie stepped out the back door.

It was raining, as usual. Seattle was a fine town, other than the rain and the fact that normal people couldn't afford the rent. Under the protection of the awning, she rummaged for her umbrella in her handbag and realized she'd left it at home.

"Where are you?" Alissa asked, as she scanned the cars and trucks in the mostly empty parking lot.

"Just two from you," Millie said. "My car broke down last week, so I bought a new one. Not that I could afford it with tuition due, but I have to get around."

"I hear you," Alissa said. "I'm worried I'll need to do the same soon. Last week, mine wouldn't start and I panicked."

"How's Sophie?" Millie asked, as they made a run for their cars.

Everyone knew the story of Sophie's accident. They'd all been rooting for her recovery.

"She's much better." Rain pelted Alissa's face and drenched her hair. She really should have worn a coat. Spring in Seattle was temperamental. Cherry trees bloomed in brilliant pink, but the days were as cold and damp as they had been for months. "They let her out of traction finally. She's home but still not able to get around much. The physical therapist will help once the casts come off but that's another month away."

"What a nightmare."

"It has been, yes."

They were at Millie's car by now. "Does that mean another month for you here?" Millie asked.

"At least."

"You're a good friend," Millie called out, as they parted ways for their cars. "Sophie's lucky to have you."

Alissa thanked her and sprinted the rest of the way to her car. Once inside, she locked the doors and waved to Millie that she was good. She set her bag on the passenger seat and wiped her face with a tissue she kept in the console. Shivering, she blinked as Millie's lights illuminated the interior of her car. She put the key in the ignition and turned. The car's engine sputtered. She cursed and tried again. Same sputtering sound. The engine would not turn over. One more time, she turned the key. Nothing.

She smacked the steering wheel. Rif or Marty would have to give her a ride home—but they were probably thirty minutes away from closing up for the night. She sighed, weary and feeling a tiny bit sorry for herself. Okay, a lot sorry for herself. All she wanted was her bed.

A tap on the passenger's-side window caused her to jump, then scream. A face appeared, blurred by the rivulets of rain down the window.

Jed Marsh. She could just make out his square jaw and dark hair. If he was a serial killer, she was about to find out.

She cracked the window. "You scared me half to death," she blurted out, her heart still pounding hard in her chest.

"I'm so sorry," he said. "I forgot my overcoat and had my driver circle back to pick it up after we dropped the guys at the hotel downtown."

She narrowed her eyes. His hair was completely wet. Droplets of water pooled on his long, black coat. Even with his dark locks plastered against his forehead, he was the most handsome man she'd ever seen.

"I'm Jed Marsh, from earlier. I was at your table."

"I remember," she said. "It was mere minutes ago."

"Right." He wiped water from his eyes as the rain continued to pound him.

"What can I do for you?" Did he think she was the type of girl who offered her services for a fee? How dare he think so, just because she worked at Rif's. "I'm not for sale, in case you wondered."

His eyes widened in what she could only interpret as horror. "What? Oh my God, no. I didn't wonder that. Not at all. What did you think? I was about to proposition you?"

She lifted a shoulder. "Why else would you show up at my car and frighten me out of my mind?"

"I noticed your car wouldn't start. And wondered if I could help. Or give you a lift home?"

"One of the guys can take me home," she said.

He hesitated, glancing toward the entrance. For the first time, she noticed a limo parked near the front of the club. "May I come inside? I'm getting soaked out here."

Please, Jesus, don't let him be a killer. She nodded and unlocked the door. He slipped inside, shivering. She became conscious of the worn cloth seats and ugly plastic dashboard.

"What seems to be the problem?" Jed asked. "I mean, with the car." He smelled so good, like vintage shaving cream. The kind her father had shaved with. When she was small, she'd sat on the closed toilet and watched him shave. She remembered the cold ceramic against the backs of her thighs.

"It won't start," she said. "She's old and tired."

That made him smile. "Does she have this problem often?"

"Just last week. But then she started again, so I put off putting her in the shop. It's so much money every time I take the old lady in."

"I don't know anything about cars, but I can have Thomas drive you home," he said.

"Thomas?"

"My driver."

"Oh, right. That's your limo?" She gestured to the long black car.

He pushed his dripping hair away from his face. "The limo isn't mine. We just rented it for the night. Those guys I was with own a high-end restaurant conglomerate and wanted to paint the town, so to speak. I'm not the type to frequent clubs."

"I had a feeling." Should she be offended?

"Not that there's anything wrong with it." His hands fidgeted in his lap. "Those ladies are very talented."

She laughed despite wanting to dislike him because of his limo and manicured fingernails. "They are."

"You carry that tray like nobody's business. I couldn't help but notice the muscles in your arms." He flushed and shook his head as he looked away. "Sorry. I'm not sure why I just said that." He shivered again.

"Are you cold?" she asked.

"Very. You?"

"Yeah."

"Please, let us take you home. The limo is nice and warm. I even have a few towels in there."

"Okay, I guess so. You're not going to murder me, are you?"

"Definitely not. Thomas won't either." He smiled as he ran both hands through his wet hair. "I'll just wave him over."

While they waited for the limo to arrive, Alissa texted Rif to let him know she'd gotten a ride home. She didn't want them to worry when they saw her car.

Seconds later, the limo came their direction. The driver, Thomas, dressed in a black suit, got out of the limo and opened the side door for them. Next thing she knew, she was seated across from Jed Marsh. She'd never been in a limo before tonight. This one had black leather bench-like seats along both sides. To her, leather smelled like money. Plastic bottles of water were tucked into cup holders. A container of Marsh Vodka nestled in a bucket of ice.

"Where to, Miss Mann?" Jed asked.

"How do you know my last name?"

"I asked Rif," he said. "I've known him for years. Because of work."

She gave him the address of her apartment. Jed knocked on the window that separated Thomas and the rest of the limo. The glass came down, and Jed passed on the information to him.

"Yes, sir," Thomas said. "Shall I turn the heat up?"

"That would be wonderful," Jed said. "Thank you."

Alissa took the dry towel he offered and patted her face and hair. Jed did the same, rubbing his head with the towel like he'd just gotten out of the shower. Messy, damp hair made him seem younger and more approachable.

"I thought you'd be a Seattle-proper kind of girl," he said.

She raised one eyebrow. "Do you think I'd be working at a club if I could afford Seattle?" She lived in an apartment building near the elementary school where she worked.

"Rif told me you're a kindergarten teacher. In addition to your waitressing job."

"That's correct."

He wrapped his towel around his neck. "Would you care for a drink? Something to take the chill off?"

"I'm not much of a drinker," she said.

"Not even when offered the finest vodka ever made?" He shed his coat, revealing his expensively tailored blue suit. After folding his overcoat in two and placing it on the seat, he shrugged out of his suit jacket. The same neat folding and tucking away hinted at an orderly, tidy man. She liked that in a person.

"I love your modesty," she said.

He laughed and reached for the bottle. "I'll add some flavored sparkling water to it if you like." The muscles of his thighs pressed against the fabric of his pants.

She swallowed, trying to focus. "I didn't say I wanted any."

His eyebrows shot up. "Sorry, you're correct. I'm usually a better listener. You're so pretty you make me nervous."

She could say the same about him. But she wouldn't. He probably heard the same line from a lot of women. This was a man who had it all—good looks, wealth, obvious intelligence. She didn't need to feed his ego by letting him know how attracted she was to him.

"If you don't mind, I'm going to have a little," he said, as he poured a small amount into a tumbler, then added ice.

She watched as he brought the glass to his mouth and took a sip. "I guess I'll have a little."

"Great." He opened one of the flavored waters and poured it into a glass, followed by a small amount of vodka.

She took it from him and stared into the rising bubbles before indulging in a dainty sip. All she could taste was the flavored water. "Not bad."

"Thank you. Family recipe that goes back to the bootleg days."

"Really?"

"I'm afraid so. I come from a line of criminals." He grinned.

"Not now, though?"

He laughed. "No, we're legit since prohibition ended. Our distillery has been making hand-crafted vodka and gin since before it was faddish to do so."

"And you work with your father?" she asked.

"That's right. He's grooming me to take over in a few years." For the first time, his sparkling eyes dimmed. Only for a second though, as if he didn't want her to see any crack in his positive exterior.

The limo sped up. They must have entered the freeway. This time of night there wasn't a lot of traffic.

"Is that what you want?" she asked. "To take over the family business?"

His eyes lifted toward the ceiling before coming back to rest on her. "I don't think about it much. It's what's expected of me."

"What do you study in school to ready you for running a gin joint?"

"It's technically called a distillery." He smiled and sipped his drink. "Business. That's my degree anyway."

"From UW?"

"No. Harvard."

She almost spit out her drink. "Harvard. Well, that decides it. You're too smart for me."

"I suspect it's the other way around. My father and grandfather went to Harvard. They're also major contributors to the school. I can't say I got in on merit only."

Was he simply acting humbly, or did he believe that to be true? She knew a little bit about not feeling good enough or as smart as the people around her.

"How about you? Where did you go?" he asked.

"I graduated from Western Washington. They have a good teaching program."

"Is that what you always wanted to do?"

She nodded, remembering when the idea had first come to her. It had been the year after her parents' death and her teacher, Mrs. Calder, had been so kind and nurturing to her, letting her stay after school to help prepare art and science materials. Mrs. Calder was young and pretty. Alissa had admired her so much. *One day*, she'd thought, *I want to be a teacher*. She'd decided later she wanted to be a kindergarten teacher. Children were little and fragile at that age. With Alissa's quiet personality, she knew younger children would be the best fit for her. "It's pretty much what I always planned."

"What made you sad just now?" He poked the tip of her shoes with his.

She looked at him over her drink, surprised. "Did I look sad?"

"The eyes always give a person away."

"My parents died when I was ten. The year after that I decided I wanted to be a teacher. Those two thoughts go together, which is why I looked sad." The vodka was going to her head and making her lips loose. She never told strangers this much information.

"I'm sorry. I can't imagine how hard that must have been."

"I miss them every day. Still, even after all these years."

"What happened?' he asked. "I'm sorry. You don't have to tell me."

"No, it's okay. I can talk about them. I like to, actually. I mean, not the way they died, but just that they were here with me for my first ten years of life. I loved them very much. Just because they're gone doesn't mean they're not my parents still. Does that make sense?" Too much of an explanation. Jed Marsh and his sympathetic eyes were upending her.

"Yes, absolutely it does."

"They died in a car accident. I was with them, but I wasn't hurt. I always think about that—I came out of there without a scratch. It's made me both apologetic and extremely interested in making the most of my life by giving to others."

"Where did you go after they died?" He leaned closer, as if he wanted to touch her.

She wished he would. "I was adopted by a wonderful woman. Maddie took me and three other girls into her home and her heart. Just like that I was part of a big family."

"That sounds nice." He loosened his tie. "I'm an only child."

"I would've been, I guess, had my parents not died. We're all super close. A bunch of stray cats all thrown together. My sisters are super special. Accomplished and successful. They'd never have to work two jobs. I'm the dummy of the group."

"Working two jobs doesn't mean you're not accomplished. School teachers should be paid more."

"You're sweet to say so," she said.

He didn't say anything, just stared at her, as if he couldn't decide if she was for real or not.

"What?" she asked.

"You're unusual, that's all."

"Unusual good?"

"Very good." He further loosened his tie. "What're you doing at that club?" he asked. "For real."

She explained about her student loans and then Sophie's accident. "I make more during my weekend shifts than I make in a week teaching."

"That isn't right."

She smiled at him, hoping to coax the frown from his face. "It's not but who said anything about right or fair? I get paid to run around in my skivvies and bring drinks to guys like your client. Men still run the world, Jed Marsh."

"Men like my father."

"I suppose you could say that, yes," she said. "But I don't spend time feeling bitter about what isn't in my control. What I can do is save my friend from financial ruin by slinging some drinks, so that's what I'll do."

"Does your family know about your job at the club?"

She shook her head. "No. They wouldn't approve of me running around in my bathing suit serving drinks. My principal at the elementary school doesn't know either."

"Is it weird having a secret like that?" he asked.

"Yes." She took a moment to find the right words. "There's this whole part of my life I can't share with them. I mean, Rif and Marty and the girls are true friends who look out for me. I wish I could tell Mom and the girls about them, but I can't. I can't take the look of disappointment in their eyes."

The car slowed and came to a halt. They were probably stopped at the light that turned onto Highway 202. She lived in a suburb called Sammamish. Soon, they'd pass through downtown Redmond, then turn right on Sahallee Way. She wished the drive would never end.

"Do you mind being an only child?" So far, they'd talked about her. He was good at asking questions, drawing her out, but she wanted to know more before it was time to say goodbye.

"I always wanted siblings," he said. "My mother, especially, is intense. So much...too much attention and expectations. Most of the time I feel like I've failed her."

"Is she hypercritical?"

"You could say that, yes." The corners of his eyes crinkled as he grimaced. "And then there's my dad. He's one of these old-school types, who parents like a football coach. Not the good kind like Pete Carol, but the ones who yell and bully their team into submission." He tugged on his ear and looked away. "Anyway, enough about that."

"Did he physically bully you?" she asked, too curious to keep her mouth shut.

"Sometimes he roughed me around, yes. Nothing serious. Just some boxing of the ears, that kind of thing."

"That's awful. Children should never be hit."

He smiled gently. "Nah, he made me tough."

"What's it like working with him?" She imagined working for a man like that would be rough for anyone, but especially for a son.

He rattled the ice around his glass. "Hard."

"I'm sorry."

He lifted his gaze to look at her. "I must sound like a monster."

"Why would you say that?"

"Poor little rich boy with mean parents, who has his own driver and a business worth millions of dollars."

"Money has nothing to do with how good a person's life is or isn't." She touched her fingertips to his knee before snatching them away. Why had she touched him? Who was she right now? So free and talkative and touching a man she didn't know. *But you do know him*, a voice in her head whispered. *You've known him all your life.* "The only thing that matters is supportive family and friends."

He watched her without moving a muscle. "Do you really think that's true?"

"I do." Transfixed by his gaze, she also froze. A current passed between them.

After a few seconds, he broke the silence. "Sometimes, I

think about walking away from it all—giving up my place in the business and going out on my own. But to do what? I'm not really good at anything except nurturing client relationships."

"Aren't there a lot of jobs like that?" she asked. "Businesses who need good salespeople?"

"I suppose. I don't know. I've felt like there are no choices in my life that haven't already been made."

"There's always a way to reinvent yourself." She touched his knee again. This time his hand covered hers before she could snatch it away.

"Will you have dinner with me tomorrow night?" he asked.

She pulled her hand back to her own knee. "I can't. I have to work."

"Sunday then?"

She looked at his earnest, sweet face. Where were the red flags she usually got with men? Nothing but white flags, one after the other.

"Yes, I'll have dinner with you on Sunday."

"Rif's ordered me to send flowers tomorrow, which I will do for the privilege of taking you to dinner."

"Rif worries too much."

"I like knowing there's someone looking out for you there." He flapped his hands apologetically. "Not that you need a man to do that for you."

"I don't, but I get your point." She smiled to ease his mind.

The car turned. Soon, they'd be at her apartment. She didn't want the night to end. How was that possible when she'd only just met him?

"What's your favorite flower?" he asked.

"Tulips." They'd been her mother's favorite. One of her fondest memories was going to the tulip festival with her parents. Rows and rows of reds, yellows, purples, as far as the eye could see.

"What color?"

"Any will do, but I love pink," she said.

"Good to know."

The sound from the car's engine changed. They were climbing the hill toward downtown Sammamish.

"What's your favorite food?" he asked.

"Simple. Bland," she said. "I eat like my kindergarteners."

He laughed. "Like fish sticks and French fries?"

"Chicken fingers and macaroni and cheese, if you want to know my absolute favorite."

"I'll be sure to take you to a place with a kid's menu." His eyes sparkled, teasing her.

The car slowed and then stopped. "We're here, I guess." She set her glass over near the bucket of ice. *I wish we weren't*, she thought.

Thomas opened the car door and backed away, waiting for her to exit.

"Wait, let me help you out," Jed said. He set aside his glass, then scooted toward the door, hopping out and then offering his hand.

Once she was out of the car, Thomas disappeared back inside.

"May I walk you to your door?" Jed asked.

Her apartment building was nestled amongst a bevy of businesses, including a bank, pho shop, music store and a few others. On the first floor of her building, the café's closed sign hung in the doorway. They'd open at six—just a few hours from now—and serve mouthwatering comfort food. The smell of pancakes, maple syrup and coffee would drift up to her apartment. She pointed to the second floor of the apartments. "I'm in 2A. Above the café."

He nodded and indicated for her to go ahead. "Right behind you."

She took the stairs slowly, partly because she was exhausted and a little light-headed from the drink but mostly because she never wanted this night to end.

When they reached her apartment, she pulled her keys out of her bag and unlocked the door. She left it open slightly and turned back to say good night. His eyes glittered in the dim light from the lamppost below.

"May I kiss you?" he whispered, so softly she wondered if she'd made it up.

"Yes."

He brushed her still damp hair from her cheek. She held her breath as he brushed his lips ever so softly, like the wings of a butterfly, against hers. Despite the gentleness of the kiss, a spark of desire rushed through her. She had to hold herself back to not throw herself into his arms and demand more.

Jed was too much of a gentleman for that. "Good night, beautiful Alissa. I'll see you on Sunday." He reached into his jacket pocket and handed her his business card. "Please text and we'll work out details."

She shook her head. "How about if you just type my number into your phone?"

"If you insist." He pulled his phone from his pocket.

She rattled off her number.

He typed into his phone. "Done. I'll text you tomorrow."

"Thank you for the ride. And good night." She slipped into her apartment before she embarrassed herself by asking for another kiss.

Inside, she locked and bolted the door, then stood against it, breathing heavily, listening to his footsteps descend the stairs.

Oh my God, she thought. *I can't wait to tell my sisters and Mom about this night.*

But she couldn't unless they knew the truth about her second job. She instructed herself not to think about all of that and, instead, just bask in the moment. He'd kissed her.

They were going out to dinner on Sunday. She hugged herself and smiled. Could she have just met her future husband?

The next morning, she woke late. A light flashed on her phone. She reached for it as the events from last night rushed back to her. A text from an unknown number flashed on the screen. It was Jed. Had to be.

Can I help you get your car to the shop today?

She'd been so blissed out that she'd almost forgotten about her stupid car. She stretched, then sat up straighter to type a message back to him.

Thanks, but I'll have to have it towed to the shop.

God only knew how much that would cost.

A return text came right away. *That car might not be worth salvaging. Have you considered buying or leasing something new?*

She typed back. *Don't you need a big down payment for that? As you say, it's not like I'm going to get a good trade-in on that piece of junk.*

One of my best friends owns a car dealership. I bet he'll cut us a deal. We can get you a new car and then I'll take you to lunch.

Alissa sat there for a moment, thinking. Was it appropriate to let a man that she didn't really know help her? A new used car? How could she afford one? If she took on another shift at the club, she risked being too exhausted to give one hundred percent to her students. The only reason it worked now was that her shifts were on the weekends. She couldn't ask her mother for money, and Sophie needed every penny Alissa made now.

She would just have to take out a loan. If she continued working at the club, she could pay it down quickly. Unless something else happened. Her fate seemed to be working at the club into perpetuity.

Sure. That would be nice. I'll be ready at noon if you want to come by and get me.

I'll be there.

Jed's friend worked at a Honda dealer with both new and used cars. Jed's friend quickly talked Alissa into leasing a new Civic instead of buying, new or used. That way, she needed no down payment, and it only increased her monthly bills by a few hundred dollars. Two additional shifts a month should cover it, she reasoned to herself. She hated to work more but at least she'd have a reliable vehicle.

Her hands shook signing the paperwork. Was this the right thing to do? Please, God, let it be.

After completing the paperwork and driving off in her new car, she met Jed at a small café in downtown Redmond. They ordered sandwiches and sodas and sat at a table by the window. Outside, the rain pounded the sidewalks. A gas fireplace warmed the room, both in temperature and atmosphere.

He'd come to pick her up in a pair of faded jeans and knit sweater that clung to his muscular torso. Now, he pushed up the sleeves and drank from his soda.

She nibbled on the end of her straw, thinking about what to do with her old car.

"What's wrong?" Jed asked. "Buyer's remorse?"

"No, not that. In all the excitement, I forgot about my old girl, and that I'm going to have to pay to have it removed from the parking lot. Rif won't like it rusting away there for long." She sighed and tugged at her earring. "Just when I get ahead, something happens, and I fall behind again."

He looked away from her to the window. Was it her imagination or did he look guilty?

"I already took care of it," he said. "While you were

signing paperwork, I called a tow truck and had it hauled off to the junkyard." He reached into his pocket. "As a matter of fact, the guy gave you three-hundred-dollars for the parts." He laid three hundred-dollar bills on the table. "He's going to mail me a check, but I'll give you the cash now."

She stared at the money. "But...but that's too easy. You shouldn't have done that. I mean, we barely know each other."

He tapped the table with his fingers. "I thought you might feel that way. I mean, I thought about that after I already did it. Are you mad?"

She met his gaze. "Not mad. I'm not sure I love a man taking over my decisions."

His shoulders rose and fell. "I'm sorry. I do that sometimes. I'm very action oriented. If I see a problem, I try and fix it." He looked so crestfallen that her heart softened.

"I grew up with a single mom and three sisters," she said. "We take care of ourselves."

"I respect that, of course. But sometimes it's nice to have a friend take care of you, right? Isn't that what you're doing with Sophie?"

"You remembered her name?"

He tapped his temple. "Anything to do with you, I've committed to memory."

In spite of her uncertainty, she had to laugh. He was adorable.

"It feels different when I'm doing it for a girlfriend," she said. "A man doing it for me seems wrong somehow."

He put up his hands. "If you forgive me, I promise never to interfere in your life again."

She returned her gaze to the cash in the middle of the table. "That will come in handy. And the car payments are not as much as I thought they would be."

"I told you my guy would take care of you," he said.

"Now you sound like a gangster. Maybe that illegal moonshine is still in your blood."

He tilted his head and looked way too cute. "Do you like a guy with a little bad boy in him?"

"I do not like bad boys. Not even a little bit."

He grinned. "Then we're in business." Sobering, he leaned forward, as if inspecting her for smudges on her face. "You're beautiful. Do you know that?"

She did actually. Just then, staring into his dark blue eyes, she felt like the most beautiful woman in the world.

When Alissa arrived at work that night, there was a bouquet of two dozen pink tulips waiting in Rif's office for her, along with a note.

Looking forward to our date tomorrow night. XO, Jed

Rif, behind his desk, placed his hands over his belly. The chair creaked in complaint as he tilted backward. "He follows directions. This is good."

She sank into the battered love seat across from his desk. "You won't believe what he did." She told him the entire story, including having her car hauled off to the junkyard.

"I thought he was a good guy," Rif said. "But I wasn't sure he was good enough for you. This rarely happens, but I think I was wrong. He might be a keeper."

Still dressed in her jeans and sweater, she crossed one leg over the other and pushed back her bangs. "It was a little heavy-handed, don't you think? I've known him less than twenty-four hours."

"You young women and your rules these days," Rif said. "A man who likes you did something nice. There's nothing wrong with that. Let him court you. Make him work for it, of course, but allow some romantic gestures."

"What do you know about romantic gestures?" she asked.

His chair squeaked as he rocked back and forth. "I'm romantic as hell. Just ask my wife."

"When was the last time you sent her flowers?"

"Last week for her birthday."

She narrowed her eyes, like she did when she suspected her kindergartners were lying to her.

"I've got the receipt to prove it," Rif said.

"Fine. I'll take your word for it."

"Listen, about this car payment. You've been doing a good job around here for years. I'm not sure how you take care of the weekend crowds without breaking a sweat but you do the job of two people. I'm giving you a raise. Another three bucks an hour."

Her mouth dropped open. "Are you sure?"

"My wife hates that I make you wear that skimpy outfit, so I feel a little guilty. Yeah, I'm sure."

She sat up straighter from where she'd sunk into the cushion. "Does this mean the costume is out?"

"Don't be ridiculous. Anyway, you'd be too warm in real clothes—the way you move around here."

"Okay, well, I gratefully accept the raise, and now I have to go change into said outfit." She stood up from the couch. "What do I do about the flowers? I don't want the other girls to see them and feel bad." She couldn't remember anyone getting flowers delivered to the dressing room ever.

"I'll keep them in here. You can take them home at the end of the night," he said.

"He asked me what my favorite flower was."

"I sure to hell hope it's pink tulips."

She grinned, ridiculously happy. "It is."

He groaned and rolled his eyes. "You make sure to text me where he's taking you tomorrow, okay? Just so I know where you are, in case I have to send the police searching for you."

"Will do," she said. "And thanks for looking out for me."

"Anytime, kid."

I hope you enjoy these stories for the holidays and all year round. If so, be sure and share the news with your friends. Have a wonderful holiday season!

Below are all the books. They make wonderful gifts!

Book 1: Christmas Sisters – Prologue book

Book 2: Christmas Kisses by Judith Keim

Book 3: Christmas Wishes by Tammy L. Grace

Book 4: Christmas Hope by Violet Howe

Book 5: Christmas Dreams by Ev Bishop

Book 6: Christmas Rings by Tess Thompson

MORE BOOKS BY EV BISHOP

Writing as Toni Sheridan

The Present

Drummer Boy

Visit www.evbishop.com for information about upcoming works, to sign up for *Ev's News*, or to drop her a line. She'd love to hear from you!

ABOUT THE AUTHOR

Ev Bishop is an award-winning, *USA Today* bestselling author, best known for her small-town contemporary romance series, River's Sigh B & B. Readers describe her books as "full of humor, love and wisdom," set in places "where breathtaking scenery and the magic of love are the best medicine for the soul."

When Ev's nose isn't in a book or her fingers aren't on her keyboard, you'll find her with her family and dogs or playing outside, usually at the lake or in an overgrown garden somewhere.

She loves any and all garden related talk and work, cooking (and eating!), and making all sorts of random things – especially out of upcycled or reclaimed items.

She hopes you loved Stevie Fox in CHRISTMAS DREAMS as much as she does and that you'll catch up with her, Maddie, and the other three soul sisters, in the rest of the Soul Sisters at Cedar Mountain Lodge series.

She hopes you loved Stevie Fox in CHRISTMAS DREAMS as much as she does and that you'll catch up with her, Maddie, and the other three soul sisters, in the rest of the Soul Sisters at Cedar Mountain Lodge series.

www.ingramcontent.com/pod-product-compliance
Lightning Source LLC
Chambersburg PA
CBHW032118170626
46808CB00006B/1999